SPELL HUNTER

MIDLIFE SPELL HUNTER BOOK ONE

AMY BOYLES

LADYBUGBOOKS, LLC

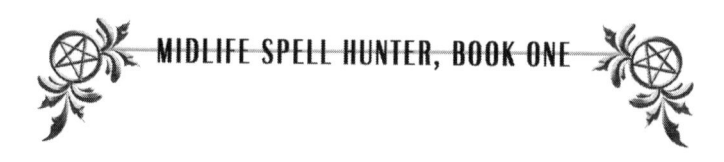

SPELL HUNTER

AMY BOYLES

CHAPTER 1

*G*eorgia Nocturne did not have any reason to expect that Dane wouldn't make it to his own party. Seeing as how it was their wedding anniversary/his birthday celebration, it made sense that her husband would carve out the time to attend.

However, Dane had a habitual problem *attending* his own parties. That was what gave Georgia pause.

There was that time his flight from Houston was delayed by three hours. He didn't make it then, of course. Oh, Georgia had a grand time reliving old stories of her and Dane and smiling and nodding at those who gave her sad looks, the sort that made her cringe on the inside.

But she had kept her chin up. It was only a party, after all.

And then there was the time when Dane got stuck in a last-minute emergency meeting at the office. It, too, had managed to outlive the party she had so carefully planned and primped for.

Once again, she cut the cake with guests who shot her sorrowful expressions.

But the worst humiliation had been last year, when Dane had actually been on his way home at five o'clock. That year he would make it, Georgia was certain. She had made sure that Dane wasn't supposed to be on any business trips. She had even prayed at every hour on the hour, doing a little begging with the big man in the sky, bargaining whatever she had so that for once, her husband would make the party that she had so carefully and painstakingly planned.

But Dane, true to form, had wound up getting into a slight fender bender on his way home and breaking his wrist.

How in the world could one man have such bad luck?

But really, wasn't it the opposite? How could one wife have such bad luck with her husband?

So this year, when it came to planning the anniversary/birthday party to celebrate Dane as an individual and them as a couple, you would think that Georgia would have plum given up.

But no, not so the case with our Georgia peach. If there is one thing that Georgia was, it was resilient.

"I'm picking up Judy from school at three p.m. and then heading to your house," Georgia's sister, Claudia, said over the Bluetooth speaker.

"No," Georgia corrected, "not three, two forty-five. That's what time kindergarten gets out."

Claudia scoffed. "It used to be three back when we were little."

"Now they let them out earlier." She took a right and swung into the elementary school's parking lot. "It's a quarter to three. Don't be too late. Judy'll think I've abandoned her."

"You should have abandoned the idea of this party, is what you should have done. The man never makes it, Georgia. Do I have to remind you of that?"

"In fact, no, you don't. But this year is going to be different." If there was ever a mantra that Georgia lived by, it was *think positive and positive stuff will happen to you.*

She supposed it was as good as any way of thinking. Besides, focusing on depressed thoughts made her feel depressed, and Georgia didn't like to be depressed. In her youth she'd taken medication for it but had weaned herself off. It had been a son of a gun to do that. So now she simply liked to keep a smile on her face and a happy attitude.

"You really think old Dane's going to make it?" Claudia said. "You sure about that?"

Georgia swung into a parking spot and killed the minivan. "Yes, I'm sure about that. He knows to be on time. There is nothing, and I mean nothing that should stop him from making it. Not even an act of God because I've been talking to him all day, offering up my next child to him if I have to."

Claudia laughed. "Your ovaries are so shriveled there's no way you're having another kid."

Georgia barked a laugh. "I resent that."

"Kid sister, you had your first one at forty. You're forty-five now. You have another kid and you'll be on the cover of *Time* as the old lady who had a kid a decade after menopause started."

"I hate you so much," she said with a laugh.

"Don't hate me. Hate the sciatica that's coming for you."

Before Georgia could respond, the car's display screen chimed that another call was coming in. "It's Dane. Let me make sure he hasn't gotten on a plane."

"See you tonight. I'll bring Judy and the vodka."

"I have enough alcohol," Georgia said.

"Not for when Dane stands you up. Again." Claudia did not hide her dislike of Dane's no-show policy. "Bye, kiddo."

"Bye. See you tonight."

Georgia switched to her husband's call and couldn't tamp down the flutter of worry in her throat. "You're okay, aren't you? Please don't tell me that you've had an accident."

Dane laughed. The sound was like buttery whiskey slipping down a throat. "Darling, I'm fine. Just fine. No accidents. I plan on making it to the party. I wouldn't miss it for the world."

"That's what you said last year."

"You could cancel."

"No," she said emphatically. "There is no way we're canceling. I've rented the space. The guests are invited. There's a *band*, Dane. We're not canceling, and if I have to drag you there myself, you're going."

His joke about not attending was not in the least bit funny. Georgia would not be made a fool of again. There would be no sorrowful looks this time. She and Dane would walk hand in hand to this party as if their lives depended on it.

But to be honest, she couldn't help the feeling that deep down, Dane didn't care—not about the party or any of it. He seemed to be phoning in on their relationship. They barely spoke at dinner, barely spoke when they got ready for their days. Half the time Georgia went to bed alone, leaving him watching television in the living room.

"What's that?" Dane said.

"I didn't say anything," she answered.

"Not you. I was talking to Rose. What's that, Rose?"

Georgia's brow hiked. "Rose?"

"She's the new secretary."

That was the first Georgia had heard of this Rose.

"I invited her to the party," Dane said. "That okay? To help her get to know others in the office."

Jealousy fired in Georgia, but she threw it away. "Sure. One more person isn't a big deal. I can't wait to meet her."

Because that's what you say when your husband's new secretary is coming to your anniversary party, isn't it?

"Listen, I've got to go. The PTA is meeting, and I need to get in there," she said.

"Have fun. See you tonight."

Georgia hung up, wondering if this Rose looked as beautiful as her name. That was when Georgia caught a glimpse of herself in the rearview mirror.

Once, one of her science teachers told her that for women, after you had a baby, your body didn't care about you anymore.

Truer words had never been spoken.

The dark circles under her eyes were a testament to that. The half-moons appeared after Judy's birth. Georgia figured they would vanish once she got a few good months of rest and added a super vitamin C concentrated eye cream to her morning and evening beauty regimens.

But the circles did not vanish. Instead they seemed to get worse.

And her upper arms! Little pockmarks of fatty tissue deposits had started to take residence in them. She added extra pushups into her exercise regimen of walking, but they still insisted on staying.

And her sister hadn't been joking about sciatica. A week ago Georgia had sat too long on one of Judy's wooden play chairs while they put together a tortuous Lego Friends play set. Now shooting pain raced down the back of her leg when she bent over.

She'd need to see her doctor about it if it didn't go away.

As Georgia peered into the mirror, she noticed the skunk-like stripe of silver that was already beginning to show on top of her head. It seemed that more and more gray appeared every day on her, while Dane didn't have any—just enough to make him look more handsome.

An age spot had also taken up residence on her right cheek. She noticed it every time she glanced in the mirror. It made her look older than forty-five.

But still her green eyes were clear and her complexion nice if you overlooked that brown monstrosity and her huge pores.

God, she was getting old.

What made it worse was that she was about to walk into a PTA meeting with a group of thirtysomethings.

Harvey Elementary School was located in a hamlet in northern Alabama. Harvey was a midsize town that had gone wet two years before. Because alcohol could now flow like a river, lots of new businesses had recently popped into existence, including a few bars. Georgia had lived in Harvey for as long as she'd been married, and she enjoyed the quiet life that it offered. Dane worked in Huntsville, which wasn't a bad commute from home.

As she gazed at the trees that were beginning to shred the shroud of winter and take on green buds, Georgia decided that there was no time like the present when it came to getting up and going to the meeting.

She grabbed her purse, exited her minivan and headed inside the elementary school.

"So we will now begin discussions on our Spring Fling," Missy Hendricks announced. "We are trying to raise funds for the electronic sign that was newly installed. It's been purchased, but we"—she placed a hand on her heart—"as the PTA do not want the school to have to foot the bill."

Missy shot a smile to Principal Brock. He was in his forties, thin, with a thick mop of brown hair. He shot Missy a look right back. It was obvious to Georgia, if not everyone in the room, that the thirtysomething Missy with her golden locks and tennis physique had a thing for Principal Brock, who apparently liked to show his dimples around the PTA president.

Missy clapped her hands together. "So, any ideas on what activities to have at the Spring Fling will be welcome." She smiled the fakest smile that Georgia had ever seen. "We have some new members present. Please don't hesitate to throw out ideas."

Georgia wasn't new, but she wasn't exactly old, either. She had joined the PTA in the fall and had attended one meeting—the one before Christmas. She had sat in the back of the small room and watched while Missy held court.

"We could do fishing for prizes," one of the women suggested.

"Great idea," Missy said. "I love it. What else?"

Georgia's phone buzzed. A text came in asking if she could find a Josephine Jones dress in size 6. Georgia was not only a housewife attempting to wrangle her husband to their party. She also sold clothing. In fact she was a Closet Holder for the Josephine Jones company. A Closet Holder was really just a fancy name for a salesperson. Georgia was active on social media selling clothing for the brand and was just about at the point where she had a few Closet Holders beneath her. That was where she would make the real money.

When she had told her sister about the part-time job that was perfect for moms, Claudia had scoffed. "Sounds like a pyramid scheme to me."

Georgia had kept her frustration to herself. After all, she had dropped a whopping thousand dollars to get her "closet" of samples— mostly children's clothing. She had sold almost all of it, but every month she had to hit certain goals to keep the percentage she made from people purchasing the clothing. If she dropped below a certain dollar amount, she would lose that percentage.

It annoyed her, but Claudia might have been right about the whole "pyramid" thing.

Georgia had not always been a housewife hustling to sell children's boutique clothing while sitting in a PTA meeting. She had, in fact, *been something* before she married.

She had been more than something—she had been someone with a life and a real job.

But whenever thoughts of her previous existence flitted into her mind, Georgia ground her teeth and shoved them aside—just like she was doing when Missy's gaze landed on her.

"And you, I'm sorry, I forget your name?"

She cleared her throat. "Georgia."

"Georgia," Missy cooed. "Do you have any ideas for the Spring Fling?"

She had one teensy-weensy idea, so she suggested it. "What if we had a small petting zoo? Just a few bunnies for the kids to hold. I'm sure we could get one of the local farmers to donate them. When we were at that farm in the fall, they had lots of bunnies. They might be interested in helping us out."

That was when Missy turned and gave Georgia a sympathetic smile that suggested her idea had been one that only a simpleton could make.

"Have you *ever been* to a Spring Fling before?" she asked Georgia in a voice that made sweat sprint onto her brow.

Georgia would not be intimidated by this thirtysomething who had nothing better to do than to make googly eyes at the principal.

"No, I haven't," she admitted.

"I didn't think so," Missy said, smiling big and wide. "We have to keep the stations moving. So we don't have time for petting zoos."

Georgia's face burned with embarrassment. This was not how being in the PTA was supposed to be. It wasn't supposed to be clicks and snotty moms. But as Missy asked others what they thought would be a good idea for stations, Georgia realized that's what this was.

Most of the women gazed at Missy with reverence, and Missy soaked it in, smiling and cooing at all their suggestions, which to Georgia's ears were stupid compared to the petting zoo.

She didn't like to be called out, embarrassed. This never would have happened in her old life—the one where Georgia was in control. But Georgia didn't feel in control. She felt like a middle-aged housewife with sagging boobs, age spots and was completely out of place in the elementary school PTA.

So that's why, as Missy continued to talk and ignore Georgia, her hand shot up and Georgia announced, "I'll get the petting zoo organized. I'll do it and it will be amazing."

Missy eyed her with a mixture of surprise and curiosity. "Well, okay then. You can organize it."

Georgia felt a rush of satisfaction. "Thank you. I will."

But that satisfaction quickly turned to mud when she realized that she had absolutely no experience with petting zoos and couldn't even remember the name of the farm they had gone to that fall.

It didn't matter. She would figure it out, and Georgia would create the best petting zoo that had ever been done in the history of Harvey Elementary School.

Or, so she hoped.

CHAPTER 2

"*W*here's Dane?" Claudia asked.

"I don't know," Georgia ground out. "He hasn't shown yet."

At the nicest downtown restaurant in Harvey, people were milling about—friends and some of Dane's coworkers had appeared, but no Dane.

Even Judy was running around people's legs, offering them drinks that she had snatched from a serving tray.

"Mama, would you like a drink?"

Judy currently held a glass of champagne. She swiped it from her daughter before the five-year-old had a chance to take a swig. "Thank you, Judy."

Judy gave her mama a big smile. "You're welcome." Then she dashed off to offer someone else a drink.

"Sip up," Claudia told her. "You look like you need it."

Dane had promised. He had *promised* not to be late, and here it was, thirty minutes after the party was supposed to begin and he hadn't called. He hadn't texted. He hadn't done a darn thing.

Georgia spotted his buddy, Brad, and headed over with the champagne flute as a peace offering.

"Brad," she said, all smiles, even though she was simmering inside her two layers of Spanx that was needed to make her glittering, waist-hugging dress look good. "Have some champagne."

Brad took it with an uncomfortable laugh. "Thanks, Georgia. Nice party."

"It would be better if Dane was here."

"Oh, he hasn't shown up yet?" Brad tugged at his collar. "I hadn't noticed."

"Cut the crap, Brad. You noticed. Heard from him?"

He checked his cell phone. "Can't say that I have."

She slid beside him and stared at the crowd that was beginning to look more confused by the minute. "Do you know something about my husband that I don't?"

"I'm afraid I don't know what you're talking about."

A couple of thoughts flashed through her mind—Dane having an affair, Dane not caring about her or her feelings. "Does my husband have anxiety about parties that I'm unaware of? He seems to have an issue with not showing up at celebrations in his honor."

Brad laughed again. It was annoying. "I don't think so, Georgia. He probably just got tied up at the office."

She pointed to the crowd. "Half of the office is here already."

"Oh, well, then I'm not sure." He patted her on the shoulder like they were buddies. "Dane'll show up. He…"

"Always does? Is that what you were going to say? No. He doesn't and you know it."

"Georgia—"

"Forget about it." She walked off, simmering. She felt like such a child, being so angry, but where was her husband?

A great whoosh of air filled the room, and Georgia pivoted, half expecting to see Dane with his hair askance and his shirt torn. He would probably claim to have just gotten hit by a car. Maybe his new name was Mayhem and he was now doing car insurance commercials.

But that's not who stood in the middle of the room.

Georgia sucked in her stomach at the sight of Demona. It was pronounced like *demon* with an *a* on the end. Not a more true name had ever been given to a person, or witch, Georgia supposed.

And that's a little secret about Georgia. She had been living for years among mortals, among humans, no less. But in reality she was born a witch, someone who can create spells and harness power for her liking.

Georgia, however, gave all that up when she decided to have a family.

But now Demona stood in the middle of her party looking ridiculously fabulous in a burgundy-colored taffeta dress. Georgia peered closer. Was that actually taffeta, a fabric for little girls? No, in fact, upon closer inspection, the dress was silk, a high-quality kind at that.

Claudia sidled up to Georgia. Her sister was a good foot taller with long blonde hair and big blue eyes. She was stick-thin, and you never would have guessed that she had any problems with middle age. She looked about twenty, though she was closer to fifty.

"What in the world is that witch doing here?" Claudia hissed under her breath.

"I'm not sure. Should we welcome her?"

Claudia scoffed. "After the way the two of y'all parted, I would surely think twice about that."

"You know as well as I do that Demona won't leave until she's said her piece."

"At least that gives you something to think about other than Dane." Georgia shot her a scathing look. Claudia lifted her hands in surrender. "Sorry, but it's true."

"Let me see what she wants."

Georgia threw back her shoulders. She would have sucked in her stomach, but thanks to the Spanx, that work was already done for her. She sailed across the room, a tight smile on her face. She would not gush and pretend to be happy to see Demona, because she wasn't.

"Georgia," Demona cooed, "is that you?"

Georgia gave the witch a stiff hug. "Let's cut the crapola. You know it's me, Demona. You wouldn't be caught dead at a party like this unless you had a reason. What is it?"

Demona's gaze flitted about the room. "And your groom? Where is he? I don't see him. What was his name again, Dane?"

"He's busy."

The witch arched a perfectly waxed chocolate-brown brow. Demona looked like perfection except for the cane she used to walk with—an old injury. There was no telling her age—sixty, maybe? But her skin was supple. Even that little crepe-like place at the base of her neck looked good. Her large brown eyes were ringed with makeup and her hair was swept up into a bun.

Georgia glanced around and noticed that all the men were watching Demona. The married ones were gazing on in curiosity, and the single ones, like Brad, watched with tongues wagging.

"Dane is busy," Georgia told her. "What do you want?"

"Already cutting to the chase, I see. That is so like you, Georgia. Nothing has changed."

Georgia didn't reply.

"You know, when we first met, with a name like Georgia, I expected you to be full of Southern charm—a real debutante."

"Sorry to disappoint."

Demona laughed lightly. "You didn't disappoint. You were one of my best spell hunters."

Georgia smiled hard to keep from exploding. "All of that is behind me now. Surely you didn't come here to talk about the good old days. If that's the case, you remind me of the high school football star whose best days were when he was eighteen."

"I have no idea what you're talking about," Demona replied.

"Of course you don't. What is it? What brings you to Harvey, crashing my party?"

Demona snatched a glass of champagne from a tray. "Fine. I'll get right to the chase." She stared at Georgia with bright eyes. "I need you."

A shock wave jolted from Georgia's spine all the way to her toes. "You need me? I'm afraid I don't understand."

That was a lie. Georgia understood perfectly well what Demona was saying, but admitting that was like admitting defeat.

Demona rolled her eyes because she, too, knew that Georgia lied. "I'm down good spell hunters. I need you to come back and work for me. I have a job, one that requires finding an elusive spell."

Georgia shook her head. "I swore that I'd never return."

"This time will be different. You'll be working solo."

"As opposed to having a partner that could be killed?" Georgia spat.

Demona smiled out into the crowd. "Now, now, dear. We wouldn't want to shout things out too loudly. The humans might hear."

Georgia couldn't believe what Demona was suggesting. "I got out of the spell hunting business, you know that. I rebuked my powers as a witch. I'm not going back."

"You were the best hunter I had," Demona said as if that would change Georgia's mind, which it did not. "It's different now. There's another group hunting the same spell, too. If it gets in the wrong hands—"

"N-O spells no."

Demona cussed under her breath. "You'll work alone. You won't be in charge of someone else."

"So if I die or end up horribly injured, it'll only be me that I have to blame myself for."

"You don't have to put it so harshly, but yes." She shook her head and sighed. "What happened to Diana was an accident. You know that."

"I was in charge of her," Georgia said bitterly.

"It wasn't your fault."

"I'm not discussing this anymore."

"You forget that Diana's safety was important to me, too," Demona said.

Guilt wormed its way into Georgia's spine. She didn't reply because what Demona said was true.

"Don't you miss it?" Demona asked. "Hunting spells at night, finding the most perfect spell that you've been searching for for days? And when you've found it, celebrating and feeling a sense of accomplishment? What are you accomplishing now in your little life—PTA bonanzas, or whatever they are, fixing supper for your husband while he lies on the couch and watches TV? Isn't that what humans do?"

Her words struck a deep chord in Georgia. The chord was plucked so hard that Georgia felt hollow inside. Yes, all those things were true. Her life had become mundane. Of course there were wonderful parts to it—Judy was one of them. But the rest—the in-between bits of her day, like when Judy was in school—were a wasteland of time spent exercising with no heart in it, cleaning the house, shopping at Target.

And now...she looked around the room. People were beginning to yawn because her husband still hadn't arrived and they still hadn't cut the freaking cake.

Demona pressed something into Georgia's hand. "My card. Call me, day or night. If you decide your life could use a little spicing up, you know where to find me."

She tipped the champagne flute to her lips. Georgia watched as the pale liquid slid into the witch's mouth. Finished, Demona handed Georgia the glass and winked before heading out the door.

Angry as a hornet in summer, Georgia laid the glass down and stared at the business card.

Claudia slid up beside her. "What did she want?"

"Me," Georgia ground out.

"In a sexual sense?"

She shot her sister a dark look. "No, of course not."

"I'm joking." Claudia folded her arms. "She wants you to work for her again, huh?"

"I'm not doing it."

Claudia sighed and stared at the door longingly. "You sure about that? Remember how much fun you had? At least, that's what you always said. I wouldn't know. You know, since I didn't get any of the witch genes."

"Consider yourself lucky. If you had, you would've been dealing with that demon."

"Oh, I don't know." Claudia swiped a glass of champagne and sipped it slowly. "You could always try it again."

Georgia's mouth dropped. "And how would I do that? I have a five-year-old."

"And an old aunt to pick her up after school," she said.

"And a husband."

"Who's late for his own party—again." Claudia glanced at her watch. "What's this? The fourth time in a row? It seems Dane really gives a whopping crap about being respectful to you."

"I'm sure—"

"Something came up?" Claudia smirked. "Something always comes up, Georgia. Don't make excuses. He's treating you like dirt, and he gets away with it."

Dane *hadn't* called or texted or anything. Claudia was right. There was absolutely no excuse for how he was acting.

Brad ran up. "Georgia, I just got a message from Dane. Apparently, there was an accident on the interstate."

Georgia's heart thumped into her throat. "Is he okay?"

"He's fine. He wasn't hurt." Brad made that annoying laugh. "He's just stuck in it."

Claudia gestured to all the people in Dane's office. "And none of them were?"

"They left before he did, I guess," Brad said.

"He should have left hours before them," Claudia murmured.

Claudia shrugged at Georgia, her gesture clear—Dane had more important things going on than making sure Georgia's needs were met.

And Claudia was right.

Fed up, Georgia clapped. "Everyone, can I have your attention?" All gazes landed on her. "Dane's been delayed. He'll be here when he can. So let's go ahead and cut the cake."

As the ravenous crowd headed for the two-tiered cake, Claudia said, "Well? You gonna call Demona?"

Georgia glanced at the card before ripping it to shreds. "Absolutely not."

CHAPTER 3

$\mathcal{B}$y the time Dane walked in, the cake was over half-eaten, most of the party guests had gone, and the restaurant manager was eyeing Georgia in a way that suggested she had overstayed her welcome—even though her time on the space didn't expire for five more minutes.

Her husband entered with his jacket tails flapping behind him. His dark hair was askew in a way that made him look annoying handsome, and his dark blue eyes were filled with worry.

"I'm so sorry I'm late," he said, swooping in to give her a kiss.

Georgia stiffened. "Don't. Just don't."

Dane rocked back, surprise on his face. "Honey, I know you're mad."

"Mad doesn't even begin to explain it." She pointed to a couch where Judy lay curled on the cushions, her hair cascading down her face, hiding it. "I planned this party for months—*months*. Everyone from your office managed to show up but you. You couldn't be bothered to leave early so that you could be on time."

He looked at her weakly. "I'm sorry. There's no excuse."

The way he surrendered made her even more angry. "You're right, there's no excuse. How could you do this? You know how hard I've planned for this, and to just act like it's no big deal is hurtful."

He wrapped her in a hug, which she moved into with her back

straight. Even though he'd been stuck in a car, Dane still managed to smell musky—it was a yummy scent that she usually adored.

"There was a traffic accident," he explained.

"I know. Brad told me. *He* knew what had happened to you, but I didn't."

"I tried calling you. You must've been in a dead spot of the restaurant." He glanced around and smiled. "Everything looks nice. You did a great job. Can I at least have some cake before you throw it at me?"

She laughed in spite of herself. How could Georgia explain that this party was about all she had beside her PTA meetings? That her life, which had once been so full, was now nothing more than waiting to drop off and pick up their daughter from kindergarten, planning what to eat for dinner, and making sure the house was clean. How could Georgia explain that everything was mundane and that she felt that she had no purpose? Yes, once you had children, you lived for them, but what about when you had a good eight hours to kill while they were at school. What were you supposed to do with that time?

They weren't rich, so it wasn't like Georgia could blow money on a country club membership and take lessons from the tennis pro. She spent her time posting on social media the newest, cutest children's outfit that had just come in and doing her best to entice the women in her network to spend their hard-earned money on said outfit so that Georgia could keep her station in the Josephine Jones company.

Since when had she become nothing more than an Avon sales lady? Because that's what she was, selling products to earn pennies. Once, she had been a spell hunter, a witch with the power at her fingertips to zap someone's rear.

And now...now Georgia was a joke. Even her husband didn't respect her. Oh, she knew that the traffic accident couldn't have been avoided. But it could have if Dane had left the office earlier—if he'd bothered to help her set up. Then he would have ensured his presence at the party. But as it was, Georgia was left making excuses for him—again.

Well, the time for excuses was over.

She crossed to Judy and roused her from the chair. "I'm taking her home. See you there." Without another word, Georgia pulled her child into her arms and left the restaurant and Dane without another word.

THE WEEKEND HAD COME and gone without much hurrah. She and Dane had spoken, but Georgi had not softened to him, not like she usually did. She was still ticked, and when he left for work that Monday morning, Georgia was glad to be rid of him.

That was when she sat down at her computer and checked her e-mails.

Georgia, we regret to inform you that you didn't hit your sales quota for the month. This means your commission will shrink. This is not something w, at Josephine Jones want to do, and so you're in luck! There is a chance to make your quota. If you can sell $1,000 worth of merchandise by tomorrow, you won't lose your coveted sales commission position.

Georgia stared at the message. Well, when it rained, it poured. She was going to lose rank. No, sales hadn't been great the past month, but to be fair Josephine Jones hadn't created any cute dress ideas. And now it was Georgia's fault that she hadn't sold enough clothing.

But there was the chance of redemption. All she had to do was sell one thousand dollar's worth of merchandise. She knew what they wanted her to do—buy the clothing herself and then resell it. That's what other women in her position did.

Anger bubbled inside her. She still simmered from the party. Dane had tried to joke with her that morning before he headed off to work, but she hadn't been in the mood. And now this with the clothing.

Georgia needed to get out of her house. She needed air. So she grabbed her purse and headed into the garage, for the minivan.

A few minutes later Georgia stood in her favorite clothing boutique downtown.

"Morning, Georgia," Hattie Williams said when she entered. Hattie was a sweet little old lady with white hair. She always baked cookies and brought them in to snack on. "Come here and see what I've got today."

And if Hattie liked you, she gave you one of those cookies. Georgia peered over the counter. There sat a covered plate. When Hattie pulled the dish towel off it, she revealed half a dozen sugar cookies.

"I've had three already," Hattie said. "It's been a busy morning. Why don't you have one?"

Georgia took the cookie and bit into it. The sugary confection melted on her tongue. She moaned. "This is delicious."

"Thank you." Hattie smiled brightly. Even her eyes twinkled. "Go on and have a look-see. Find something that'll make you feel pretty."

Retail therapy wasn't the best therapy at the moment, but it would do to make Georgia feel a smidgen better. Not that she expected to buy anything, but just looking always helped.

She ran her fingers over the new cotton blouses and ropes of necklaces that Hattie had on display, but didn't find anything that she wanted to try on.

"Something got you down today?" Hattie asked.

"Oh, just my boring old life."

The old woman smiled. "If it's so boring, make it interesting."

"Good point." She finished perusing the wares and walked back to the counter. "I didn't find anything."

"That's okay, dear. You come back anytime." Hattie winked. "You know I'll always have a treat for you."

"Thank you."

Georgia walked outside and made it about three steps when a man wearing a dark jacket, his head down, brushed past her and into the shop.

Her spine tingled. He didn't look like the sort of man who would be going into a clothing boutique. Following her instincts, Georgia turned around and headed back inside the store.

"Don't move," he growled at Georgia. "Stay where you are."

And that was when Georgia saw the gun. He had it pointed at her but turned back onto Hattie.

"Give me everything in your cash register."

Hattie scowled. "Young man, what are you doing, robbing me? I'm an old woman with a shop."

"Just shut up and give me the money," he demanded.

"Hattie," Georgia said lightly, not wanting to disturb the man, who seemed desperate. On top of that, certainly he was not thinking clearly. Why else would he be robbing a boutique instead of a gas station, a business that would obviously have more cash in their register? "Why don't you do what the man says?"

"Because I worked hard for this cash and he has no right to just walk in here and ask for it," Hattie said with a snort. "This is my money. If he wants it, he's going to have to take it."

In Georgia's life there had been very few times since she'd given up her magic that she wanted it back. This was one of them. If she had her power, she could easily zap the gun straight from his hand. But as it was, Georgia found herself staring, helpless to do anything except attempt to talk an ornery old woman into going the easy way out and not getting hurt.

The man waved his gun. "Come on! I don't have all day! Give me the cash or I'll shoot, lady. I'll do it."

Fear spiked down Georgia's spine. "Do as he says."

Hattie glared pure hatred at him. "I will not. If you want my money, you'll have to shoot me to get it."

"Hattie, no," Georgia said. She quietly circled closer to them. Maybe she could lunge at the robber and knock the gun from his hand.

Sweat poured down his forehead. He'd only come here to rob, not to shoot an old woman, Georgia thought.

She opened her own purse. "Here. Take what I have. I've only got about twenty dollars, but you can have it."

The man sneered and stuffed it in his pocket with a quick flick of the hand. "Now, old lady, give me that money."

Hattie stared at him in challenge. "If I told you once, I told you a thousand times, I ain't giving up my money. You'll have to shoot me to get it."

"I don't want to shoot you."

"Then give me that gun." Hattie reached over and grabbed the barrel. "Hand it over!"

"Let go," he demanded.

Georgia didn't know what to do. Get in the middle of them and be shot? Attack him and he might accidentally shoot Hattie. He might accidentally shoot her anyway.

She had to get that gun. That was most important. Georgia darted toward the man, mouth open to bite his hand because she couldn't think of another means to stop him.

That was when the gun exploded.

Everything stopped. The robber backed away, his voice shaking. "I didn't mean it. I swear, I didn't mean it. Why didn't you just give me the money, lady?"

With that, he dashed from the boutique. Georgia glanced over at Hattie. Blood seeped through her blouse at the shoulder. She stared at Georgia, wide-eyed.

"I do believe I've been shot. Georgia, will you call an ambulance for me?"

Those were Hattie's last words before she slumped to the ground.

"WE'RE MOVING Mrs. Williams to the ICU," the doctor told her. "She's not stable. The next twenty-four hours will be critical."

Georgia's stomach seized at the news.

Hattie had been taken to the emergency room in an ambulance. Georgia had followed in her car. Since she didn't know any of Hattie's relatives' phone numbers, she thought it best that someone should be with the woman in the hospital.

Luckily one of the neighboring shop owners did know how to contact Hattie's son, and said she would do that.

But he hadn't arrived yet at the hospital, so Georgia was the doctor's contact—and she shouldn't have to be the one to hear this.

She raked her fingers through her hair. "Will Mrs. Williams be okay?"

He scratched his salt-and-pepper hair. "She's lost a lot of blood. We gave her an infusion, but her vitals are still unstable. However, Mrs. Williams is stubborn. The good thing is, the bullet went straight through and didn't hit any bone. But she's also older. A physical shock like this is harder on the elderly."

Georgia nodded dumbly. "Thank you." What else could she say? Of course she wasn't thankful for the news, but it wasn't the doctor's fault that Hattie might die.

Good grief. If only Georgia had had her powers. Then none of this would have happened.

Tears pricked her eyes, but Georgia refused to cry.

If she'd been able to use her magic, Hattie never would have been shot. The man never would have gotten away. He would have been arrested and charged for attempted robbery. Because that's what it would have been—*attempted.*

But it hadn't been attempted at all—it had been a cluster-funk.

As Georgia sat in the waiting room listening to the sounds of those around her, people coughing and murmuring to one another, she asked herself if the track she had chosen in life was the right one.

Days earlier, she'd been sure. But now, with Judy in school, things were different. She had plenty of time to herself in the middle of the day. And she wasn't Dane's number-one priority. She couldn't even think of him right now, because Georgia was thinking of the one person she had pushed aside for ten years—*herself.*

It was time for a change. This life, the one she had signed up for, wasn't cutting it. There was another option, one where Georgia wasn't powerless when strangers tried to rob old ladies.

"Are you here for Mrs. Hattie Williams?"

Georgia glanced up into the face of a man about her age with dark hair. "Yes. You're her son?"

He nodded and sat beside her. "Yes, Dow Williams. Got here as soon as I could. What's the news?"

Georgia took his hand and proceeded to tell him what she knew. When she was finished, she left to do something she never thought that she would do—reclaim her magic.

CHAPTER 4

"*A*re you sure that you're doing this right?" Claudia asked.

Georgia sat in her kitchen with a mortar and pestle, some herbs, a sharp ritual knife with a leather-wrapped handle and an S-shaped blade.

In fact, she was not sure at all if she was doing this right, but a person had to start somewhere.

"This is how I sealed off my power," Georgia said. "So surely the same ritual will call it back."

Claudia looked at her skeptically. "You got rid of your magic for a reason."

"Because I was stupid enough to believe in fairy tales, and that witches couldn't be married to mortals. Well, now I want it back."

"You're sure about this?"

Mostly was the answer that popped into Georgia's head. It wasn't an answer that Claudia would like. Claudia liked for things to be one hundred percent certain. To Georgia, eighty percent certainty was close enough.

"Yes, I'm sure. I want my powers. Claudia, I could have stopped a woman from being shot today."

Claudia nibbled her bottom lip. "I understand that. But you were *so* sure when we did this the first time—when you asked the goddess to take your powers. You *knew* that was what you wanted."

"And now an old woman is in critical condition. If that's not a wake-up call, I don't know what is. I should have been able to stop it, Claud. It never should have come to her being hurt. I don't even know if she'll survive."

"You have the son's phone number so that he'll keep you updated?"

She thought of the slip of paper tucked into her pocket. He'd written his name on the torn-off back of a hospital pamphlet about diabetes and penned his number on it.

"I'll call him tonight and see how she's doing. For now we have to focus on this—on me getting my powers back."

Claudia glanced into the mortar. "Doesn't look thick enough. I think you need more of that dark stuff over there." She pointed to a cloth bag filled with charcoal.

"You're right," Georgia said, adding more and grinding it with the pestle. "How does that look?"

"Better." She paused. "Shouldn't we be doing this ritual at night with the full moon instead of before kindergarten pickup?"

It was a good point, but if there was one thing that Georgia had learned when it came to children, it was that you took your opportunities when you could get them.

"The next full moon isn't for another week, and I refuse to wait that long," Georgia countered. "So." She lifted the mixture and presented it to her sister. "Will you help me or not?"

She shook her head sadly. "I'll help you."

"Without judgment?"

"Without judgment. I just know how much you wanted to be the way you are. Going back…you left that life for a reason."

She had left because of guilt, because she had allowed someone to be hurt on her watch. Well, someone had been hurt again. Besides, all signs were pointing to yes, that it was high time she returned to the life she had left.

"Everything will be fine," Georgia said in a soothing voice. "Now. Smear that goop on me while I beg the goddess to give me back my powers."

24

Claudia lifted the pestle that had black goo dripping down the side. "Your wish is my command."

As her sister swiped the substance on Georgia's forehead and arms, she began to pray to the goddess, asking for her powers to be restored. The prayer itself possessed some magic, and as she spoke, Georgia felt a tingle in her gut.

"All done," Claudia said.

"Hand me the knife."

That was the part Georgia looked forward to the least. She didn't particularly want to cut herself. Pain was never fun. But the slicing and dicing of her flesh was essential to the ritual.

She lifted her shirt and moved the blade over the air, mimicking the movement that she would make for real, in only a few moments.

"Ugh. That is going to hurt," Claudia said encouragingly.

Georgia glared at her sister. "You don't have to remind me or rub it in, making it worse."

"I don't think anything that I say could make cutting your own abdomen worse. It's ironic, don't you think? That the seat of you power is basically just over your ovaries?"

"I hate you ever so much, sister."

Claudia puckered her lips and kissed the air. "But I love you so much, dearest sister."

"If you're through distracting me, I would like to get this over with."

"Proceed. I will be here with gauze and a huge bandage." She brandished both proudly. "Now, go on and do it. Your daughter is not going to pick herself up from school."

Georgia glanced at the clock. It was already two. She did need to boogie. "Goddess, here goes nothing."

She sliced the blade over her flesh and immediately felt the stinging bite. Georgia clamped down her teeth and murmured the chant through her nearly pursed lips.

Finishing, she said, "Goddess, if my intentions be true, please restore what was once mine."

She dropped the knife and heard it clatter to the floor.

"Well?" Claudia applied antiseptic and Neosporin to her wound. She then pulled the backing off the bandage and slapped it ever so gently onto Georgia's belly. "Do you think it worked?"

Georgia did a mental check, probing around for her power. Used to be, she could feel it coiled in her belly like a snake, ready to strike.

But now, nothing.

The defeat deflated her. "No, I guess it didn't work. I suppose the goddess doesn't think that I should have it back. I guess I'm not worthy."

"Oh, hon."

Claudia wrapped her in a hug that proved a bit too tight. "My stomach," Georgia said, wincing.

"Sorry. Well, let's get that mud off your face and get you looking presentable."

"Okay."

It surprised Georgia exactly how disappointed she was not to receive her powers back. But it was her own fault. When you give something up, you can't ask for it to be returned.

She followed Claudia to her bathroom. "Yeah, let's get me cleaned up."

GEORGIA FELT ABSOLUTELY no power when she picked Judy up from school. Nor did she feel a stir in her gut as she made a quick supper of spaghetti and salad.

It wasn't until she, Judy and Dane were seated at dinner and she had just swallowed her first bite of food since the ritual that power swirled in her gut.

Dane shot her a worried smile across the table. "How's Mrs. Williams doing?"

"I talked to her son just before dinner, and he said she's in stable condition."

That was something to be happy about. But what wasn't to be happy about was the fact that her water glass was suddenly trying to levitate.

Georgia snatched it from the air before anyone noticed.

"I'm sorry again about the other night," Dane said sheepishly.

"Why are you sorry, Daddy?" Judy asked, her mouth stained orange from the sauce.

Georgia's anger at Dane had softened. There was nothing like a good-old near-death experience to lessen anger and also make a gal attempt to get her magic returned to her.

Speaking of—Georgia's fork was now lifting from its place on the plate. She quickly snatched it, and now held both her fork and glass.

"I can't believe something like that would happen in our town in the middle of the day," Dane said, brows narrowed. "It makes no sense. We live in a safe place. I'd hate to start thinking of moving."

Georgia eyed her plate fearfully. "I don't think we have to consider moving. It was a fluke. I'm sure it won't happen again."

"Yes, but Hattie is an old woman." Dane rose and grabbed Judy's empty plate. "Would you like more, dumpling?"

Their daughter shot him an orange-toothed smile. "Yes, sir."

"Such good manners," he said softly before walking to the stove and fixing seconds for them both. "What about you, Georgia?" He eyed his wife, who still held her fork and glass and who watched her plate as if it were going to snap at her. "Are you okay, honey?"

"Yes!" She jumped up and raced to the sink, placing her fork and glass in the basin. Then she darted back to grab her plate and do the same. "I'm not hungry. Look, there's something I remembered. I've got to run to the…hospital."

"At this hour?" Dane looked perplexed. "Can't it wait?"

She only needed to say two words for him to back down. "The party."

He smiled genuinely. "Go do what you need to. I'll clean the kitchen and get Judy bathed and ready for bed."

"Aw, I don't want to take a bath," Judy griped.

Dane glanced at her sternly. "Unless you want to look and smell like a jar of spaghetti sauce tomorrow at school, I suggest you take a bath."

Judy made a face of distaste, but Georgia hardly noticed. She already had her keys in hand. "I'll be back soon!"

Within seconds she was out of the house, in the garage and starting up her minivan. She drove a few blocks and stopped, exhaling deeply.

Georgia looked at her shaking hands. "My goddess. She gave them to me! She returned my magic!" She sighed dramatically. "Now I just have to remember how to control it. The best way to do that is practice. And I know just the place."

Five minutes later Georgia had parked in the lot of the town's public children's playground. It was a perfect spot to explore her new powers —empty and full of potential.

She headed over to the swings. The problem that she had experienced at dinner was a buildup of energy. The goddess had indeed given Georgia back her power, and she'd juiced her up, so to speak. All the magic had returned in an instant, creating a weird sort of magical feedback loop.

The only way to stop the loop was to blow off some steam.

Georgia rubbed her hands together. "This should be fun."

She zapped a swing and sent it flying up and around the pole until it wrapped itself up, making anyone unable to use it.

"That won't do at all, will it?" she whispered. Georgia sent a line of magic to the swing, and it unwound itself but did not stop at the bottom. It kept going until it was once again wrapped around the beam again.

"What the heck?" That was not supposed to happen. The swing, as she had commanded her power, was to stop when it reached its original position.

But it had kept going. Georgia decided that she'd used too much juice. That was all. It had been so long since she'd harnessed her magic that she found herself overcompensating. This was an easy fix. All she had to do was pull back on how much power she used.

Deciding the swings had royally ticked her off, Georgia moved on to the seesaw. This she could manage. Just a whisper of magic in the seesaw's direction should get it moving.

Easy peasy, lemon squeezy.

Georgia aimed her finger at the structure and sent what she thought was a tiny fraction of magic straight at it. Her power touched the seesaw, moving along it like electricity. The next thing she knew, the thing had launched into the air and landed fifty feet away, breaking in two.

"Holy cow. I don't think I'm in Kansas anymore." She stared at her hands. "What is going on with me? None of that was supposed to happen."

"I'll tell you what's going on."

Georgia whirled around to find Demona standing beside the swings.

"What do you want? Did you follow me? Desperation is really not a good look on you, Demona."

The witch smirked. "You're the one who looks desperate, sending a children's playground toy flying into the air."

"It was an accident."

"I'm sure it was. You can't help it. I know all about that."

Goddess, she hated to ask Demona for help of any kind, but the witch said she had an answer. "So tell me—what's going on?"

Demona smirked and took a step forward with the help of her cane. She wore another taffeta-like dress, but this one was royal blue. What was up with all the shiny outfits?

"What's going on with you, child, is that you've regained your powers near menopause. Your body is changing, and so is your magic."

Georgia hated to ask but said, "What exactly does that mean?"

Demona smiled. "Come with me, and I'll tell you everything."

CHAPTER 5

Georgia followed Demona in her minivan to a diner. It was the sort of place that only took cash and served hamburgers that were coated in flour and deep-fried.

Yep, that was a thing.

"What do you know about my magic?" Georgia asked. She did not like being with Demona. Yes, at one point she had trusted the witch, but many years had passed since Georgia had worked for her. Demona reminded Georgia of decisions she had made—bad ones, the sort that got people hurt.

Demona ripped off the top of two sugar packets and dropped the granules into her coffee. "What I know is that without me, you'll be in trouble."

"I doubt that."

She tsked. "My dear, you haven't had your powers in years, and suddenly you did what—asked the goddess to return them right when you're going through *the change?*"

There were so many things that Georgia hated about that phrase. "I might have done that, yes," she admitted.

"Well, that was your mistake." Demona sipped her coffee. "If you had never rebuked your gift and let menopause—"

"Please don't say that word. That is an old-lady word."

"And how old are you, my dear?" Demona eyed her pointedly.

"Not that old."

She scoffed. "Tell your body that, then. But as I was saying, if you had kept your magic, then all these little jumps would have been controllable."

Even as Demona spoke, the silverware on the table rattled. Georgia worried her hands, hoping to stop the magic leaking out of her.

Demona continued. "But you did everything that you shouldn't have. You got rid of your power when you should have kept it, and you've secured it now, when your body is on a pathway of great change. So is your magic. It's exploding out of you. You can't control it. I can help you—for a price."

"Here it comes," Georgia griped. "What you really want."

"What I want is for you to be a successful witch. That is all. Now. There is a little trick that I can put on you, a bit of a binding spell that will help. But it won't last more than a half a day."

Georgia cocked a brow. "And the other half of the day?"

Demona's lips curved into a triumphant smile. "Why, the other half of the day, you work for me."

"Doing what?"

"Do I really have to tell you?"

Georgia frowned. "I'm not a spell hunter."

"Then why did you regain your magic?"

Georgia had no answer. For in fact, she had given the idea of returning to Demona a flirting thought. Then Demona had to go and ruin it by acting as if it was already a done deal.

"For your information," Georgia said, "I regained my magic because with it, I could have saved an old woman from getting hurt."

"Ah," Demona said, "the same thing that made you leave your magic behind is why you begged the goddess to restore it."

Georgia's stomach twisted sourly. "I don't want to talk about that."

"But talking is how we get through things. Unless you'd rather store your feelings away and throw yourself into other pursuits—such as being a mother and wife. By the way, I never did see your husband the other night. Where was he?"

"He got in a car accident. Sorry, no. He wasn't in one. He got stuck in the traffic jam after one." Why was she explaining herself to a woman who hadn't been in her life for years? "I don't have to tell you anything."

Demona reached out and took Georgia's hands. "My dear, you need to heal. You thought that by simply forgetting what had happened, that it would make the pain go away. You thought that you could toss aside your power, marry a man, have a baby and be so busy with raising her that you would forget the hurt that is in your heart. That your confidence would somehow be magically restored. But that isn't what happened. All you did was hide it away, tuck it down into a secret place where it festered. I can tell you right now that Diana would want you to keep going."

Georgia stiffened. "I failed her. I failed you," she whispered.

"You did not fail me. You think that's true, but it isn't. And as it goes, you have the chance to make it up. You really want to get out of this path that you're in? Make a change in your life? Do something besides going to PTA meetings filled with women who look down on you?"

Georgia's eyes widened. "How do you know that?"

"Because, my dear, you are an outsider. You are a witch, and that makes you different. Others may accept you, but there will always be something a little off about that acceptance. Also"—she leaned forward conspiratorially—"you're in a small town. Small towns are always filled with people who've been friends for years. They don't accept others as easily as they do in big cities."

She had a point. "You can bind my power?"

A glint of amusement filled Demona's eyes. "I can. You won't need me to do it for many days. You'll get used to your power quickly enough. But I will do this, on one condition."

"I work for you," Georgia said quietly.

Demona grinned. "I have a job. There's a client looking for a particular spell, but I can't seem to find it."

"What spell is it?"

Demona glanced around. The diner was mostly empty. She didn't have to worry about anyone overhearing. Even their waitress was occupying herself on the other side of the room, wrapping silverware into napkins.

"It's a mind-control spell."

"What sort of mind-control spell?" There were all sorts out there—

slight mind control, suggestive control, etc. Demona had to be more specific before Georgia would accept the job. "I need details."

"It's a spell where if you mix enough of them together, you can have absolute control over dozens, if not hundreds and thousands of people."

Georgia exhaled low. "That's only a myth. That spell doesn't exist. I mean, there have been rumors of people finding groups of them, but I've never seen it."

Demona lifted a brow. "We have intelligence that it does exist, that there are several of them nearby. And the most telling sign is that there are other hunters searching."

"What?" Only one time in her life had Georgia encountered other hunters, and that had been disastrous.

Hunters were not only rare. They were a dying breed. The spells that they searched for were hard to find, and most witches didn't have the power of sight to search for them. Sight was the gift of the spell hunter. Once a spell hunter touched a spell (which were little colored orbs), other witches could then see it.

But only a few hunters could find the spells to begin with. And they were sneaky. Most spells had been created centuries before and were hidden in places where they could be kept safe.

Demona had not replied, so Georgia said, "There are other spell hunters?"

"Yes, and they're searching, too. I don't know who they're working for, but I have a few ideas."

"Who?" Georgia found herself getting excited. She hadn't been on a job in so long she'd forgotten how exhilarating it was to get the first bit of intel. She'd also forgotten how exciting the hunt was. When it came to searching out a particular spell, it was all-hands-on-deck until that magic was found. "Who's looking for it?"

Demona started to smile but stopped herself. Georgia knew the old witch realized Georgia was about to accept the job. It was most annoying.

Demona spoke. "The wizard Tarwick is searching."

"Who?"

"You have been out of the loop." Demona shook her head. "Tarwick has been a thorn in my side these past few years. The last time I encountered his name, the wizard was searching for an invisibility spell."

"Plenty of wizards want that."

"But they don't want to pair it with a resurrection spell."

Georgia's blood went cold. "I'm sorry?"

Demona nodded. "Tarwick wanted to resurrect a body and then cloak it so that he could have the thing do whatever it was that he wanted."

"This guy sounds bad."

"You don't know the half of it. Worse, I've never met him. No one has, so we don't know what he looks like."

An evil wizard searching for a spell and no one knew what he looked like? Oh, this could be fun.

But wait—she had Judy and Dane to think about. Georgia couldn't just run off and get herself killed. She had to think about her family.

"You're worried about your child," Demona said as if reading her mind. "You won't be lurking about at night, if that makes you feel better. You can do most of your investigating during the day, when you can see exactly who it is that's standing in front of you—or behind you."

Daylight snooping didn't sound so bad. In fact, it sounded down-right doable. This could be great. Maybe it would spark something in Georgia that Dane would see. Because she had to face it, it wasn't just that he'd missed his own party *again* that bothered her.

They were in a rut—like a deep valley sort of rut. She couldn't remember the last time they'd been intimate. It must've been…well, there was no telling. It wasn't like Georgia kept a calendar about that sort of thing.

But it wasn't just Dane's fault. Perhaps it was her age, but Georgia just didn't have any interest in doing the nasty with her husband. It wasn't because he was an overweight slob. She simply lacked desire. Must be the pre- or current menopausal hormones—or lack thereof—flowing through her veins.

But perhaps a little danger or hunting or magic or all of it would change her current status from not interested to very interested.

As she considered this, Demona watched her in a way that suggested the older witch knew exactly what was going on in Georgia's head. It was a very annoying habit. One that Georgia had forgotten Demona possessed.

And it was while Georgia was receiving this know-it-all look from Demona that she decided on the exact course of action she would take.

"I'll do it," she said. Even saying the words made her feel like a huge weight had been lifted from her shoulders.

"I knew it," Demona said, a bit too confident in her delight for Georgia's taste. "It's hard to leave the fold forever."

"On one condition," Georgia stated.

Demona arched a brow. "And that is?"

"That I can leave at any time. There is no contract between us—not like last time."

"Done."

Georgia nearly balked. It wasn't like Demona to not want a little blood offering to ensure that she kept her hunters all to herself for an allotted amount of time. Perhaps the years had mellowed the witch. But Georgia thought that too unrealistic. Demona surely had other intentions.

"You're fine with that?" Georgia said, pushing her old mentor.

Demona laughed. "Why wouldn't I be? You're doing me a favor. After all, you might find it quite difficult to juggle a family and a part-time job. Oh, wait. You already have one of those, don't you?"

"I did," she said sourly. "But I plan to quit."

"Yes, selling children's clothes online for a commission isn't exactly what you were cut out for, my dear."

"You knew about that?"

"You'd be surprised what I know." Demona rose and wiggled her finger. "There. Your power is bound until tomorrow morning at nine sharp."

Georgia relaxed and noticed that the silverware was no longer jumping. "Thank you."

"Don't thank me yet. There's a lot of work ahead of you. But don't worry—I'll triple the sum you made monthly from your pitiful pyramid-scheme job, and I'll even make sure that you're home by two so that you can pick up Judy."

Georgia stared at Demona in shock. "You know her name?"

"My dear," Demona said in that superior voice of hers, "there is very little that I do not know."

Georgia could do nothing but stare mutely.

"Now come," Demona continued. "Let's get you home before that husband of yours starts to worry."

CHAPTER 6

*B*ut it turned out that Dane wasn't worried at all. In fact, he was sound asleep when Georgia got home. So much for him being so concerned about her welfare that he'd stay up late waiting for her.

But it was fine because Judy was asleep in her room, tucked snuggly under the covers. The corkscrew curls that sprouted from her head fell in a cascading wave over her eyes. Georgia brushed them away and kissed her daughter's forehead.

"Good night, sweet angel."

She returned to her bedroom and undressed in darkness. She slid beneath the duvet and couldn't wait until tomorrow, when the next stage of her life began.

"No time for breakfast this morning," Dane said as Georgia plated three eggs for him. "I've gotta run. An early morning meeting."

He was fresh from the shower, his wavy brown hair still damp. Dane tightened his tie and smiled apologetically. "Sorry, honey. Looks like a great breakfast." He kissed her chastely on her forehead. "I should be home in time for supper, though."

A horn honked outside, and Georgia glanced out the window to see Brad's sleek Corvette pulled into their driveway.

"Brad's early today," she said, amazed.

Judy ran to the window. "Uncle Brad! I want to see him."

Dane picked her up. "I'd love for you to pumpkin, but Daddy's got to go. Uncle Brad and I have a presentation to go over." He kissed her and plopped her back on the floor. "Be back tonight! Y'all have a great day!"

Then he was gone. Out the door, and Brad was revving the Corvette's engine. Georgia watched as Dane slid into the passenger seat and then Brad hauled butt down their driveway and through the neighborhood.

"I hope he doesn't get a ticket," she murmured.

"Mama, what's a ticket?" Judy asked.

"A speeding ticket."

"Oh, then they'll have to go to jail."

Georgia nodded mutely as she wondered who was going to eat all the eggs she'd made.

The first thing she did after dropping Judy off at school was to call the Closet Holder above her at Josephine Jones and say two words, "I quit."

Her Closet Holder of course wanted to keep Georgia, but Georgia was finished working her tail off posting pictures day in and day out on social media while hustling to meet monthly quotas.

She was done, and dropping those chains from her wrists felt dang good.

It felt like freedom.

She reached Spell Hunter headquarters at eight fifty-five. Five minutes early. Demona would be pleased. The truth was, Georgia hadn't wanted to be driving when her powers started back up.

She'd hate to make her minivan levitate in midair. She would definitely have a hard time explaining to the police, much less her husband, how she had managed such a feat.

Spell hunter headquarters looked like a dump from the outside. It was located one town up from Harvey in the old warehouse district. No, Georgia had not settled far away from her old job. Perhaps in the back of her mind she had known this day would eventually come—that she'd return to the fold.

She pulled open the metal door. Its bottom scraped against the concrete pad, causing Georgia to cringe. Nope, nothing had changed about headquarters. It was all the same.

She stepped inside. A small foyer blocked her from entering. A red light shone above her, and another door, also made of metal, stood a few feet away. Past experience told her that the second door was locked.

"Couldn't even put down security for me, could you, Demona?" she murmured.

"State your name," a voice said.

Georgia folded her arms and sagged onto one hip. "Really, Toad? You're going to pretend that you don't know me? Please don't insult me and yourself."

"Oh, Georgia, I was just having a little fun." A small body complete with wings pushed its way out of the wall and fluttered in front of her. "It's good to see you."

Toad the Fairy hadn't aged a day in ten years. He was small but muscular and built, wearing regular-looking clothing. But try to enter the building and he would spit fire from his mouth, scorching whoever attempted to come in uninvited.

She extended her finger, and Toad shook it. "Glad to have you back."

"Glad to be back," she said even though her stomach twisted. "Now, are you going to let me inside?"

"Yeah, we can catch up on pleasantries later. I heard you popped out a kid."

She rolled her eyes. "That's one way to put it."

Toad rubbed his hands together. "Open salami!"

"Is that the code for today?"

He laughed. "Yep. I like it. Might use it again soon."

The metal door at the end of the hall opened, and Georgia stepped through into a room brightly lit.

Where the outside of the building was a dump surrounded by old drink bottles and newspapers that looked like stationary tumbleweeds, the inside was spectacular.

It was all clean steel lines and bright light. Even though it looked sterile, it was really quite warm with touches of red and jewel-toned cushioned chaise lounges and chairs.

It was a mixture of Bat Cave meets teenage girl's room. A strange combination, but it worked.

Demona got up from her chair. "Ah, right on time. That spell I placed on you should be crumbling any moment now. Did you have any problems with it?"

"No." Georgia shook her head. "It worked great."

"And your family? Were they safe and sound when you found them?"

Sound asleep, she thought. But as she wasn't interested in getting too close to Demona, because being too close brought up too many sad memories, all she replied was, "Yes, they were fine. Thank you. I feel my powers coming back. If you have any pointers on how to control them, I would greatly appreciate it."

Demona smiled. "That is one of the things we'll go over. Since you want to get the ball rolling, let's work on that first."

Demona led Georgia to a counter that looked like a wet bar placed in the middle of headquarters.

"Where is everyone?" Georgia asked. "Last time I was here, this place was teeming with agents."

Demona's expression darkened. "I've lost a lot in the past few years. It's only been me and Toad for a while. I can hunt some spells, but I'm not young enough to go up against Tarwick. That's why I came to you."

Fear prickled down Georgia's spine. "I'm the only agent you've got? Have the others been killed?"

"Some have retired."

"Uh-huh. And the others?"

"No one wants to be a spell hunter anymore, Georgia. Witches would rather set up soirees and create magical towns with shifters and fairies than do the hard work of spell hunting."

"That doesn't quite answer my question."

The older witch scoffed. "You are a dying breed. Those witches who can see spells are a rarity. That's why I need you. That's why you have to find the mind-control spell before Tarwick. Satisfied?"

"Not really." Demona was hiding something, but Georgia would let it slide for now, mainly because her clothing was beginning to lift obviously from her skin. Her power had returned. Demona's binding had worn off, and the magic was back with a vengeance.

"Let's work on you, then," Demona said. She pulled three rocks glasses from beneath the counter and set them on the slick steel surface. Well, what did you know? The structure was a wet bar. "I want you to lift these glasses and hold them in the air. All three of them."

Without arguing, Georgia did as Demona said. She shot out tendrils of magic that wrapped around each glass and levitated them. For fun, she even made sure the glasses hovered at an even height in the air.

"Hold it," Demona instructed, "while I talk." She moved around the counter as she did so. "When I found you last night, *you*, my dear, thought that blowing off extra power was the key to calming down your magic."

"I take it that isn't the case."

"You are such a fast learner," she teased. "No, it isn't. What you need to do is focus your power, rein it in. It is yours to master. When you feel it beginning to leak from you, Georgia, you must own it. Not be afraid of it. That's the problem with most witches. They're afraid of their magic, and it controls them. You must not let that happen. Now, you will find that your abilities are different. Menopause—"

"I would really appreciate it if you stopped saying the M word. I'm only forty-five."

Demona sniffed. "*Menopause* causes many changes in us. The main one for witches is that your power can be heightened. Hence what you're experiencing now. To control the extreme fluctuations in magic, you must focus. Do not try to blow off any excess, because that will only make matter worse."

Even as she spoke, Georgia felt her power begin to recede and quietly coil back into her. It became a thing that she controlled instead of it attempting to control her.

"There you are," Demona said with a pleasant smile. "Now, lower the glasses and we'll discuss your job."

"Do you have to keep binding me?"

Demona shook her head. "No. I believe once was all you need. You'll be fine from here on out. Just remember what I taught you."

Georgia did as instructed and followed Demona to a sitting area with a large screen placed at one end. The older witch snapped her fingers, and an orange orb with a yellow center appeared on the screen.

"That is the mind-control spell. My intelligence—"

"I thought you said there weren't any other spell hunters here. How are you getting intelligence?" Georgia challenged.

Demona smiled. "My dear, just because I'm working on a skeleton crew doesn't mean that there aren't other agents I reach out to. Satisfied?"

"Not really."

"It will have to satisfy you. This is a drawing of what the mind-control spell is supposed to look like. Some have claimed to see it, but that can't be verified. We know that the location of this spell is where you would find most other spells."

"The swampy areas near the wildlife refuge," Georgia said.

"So you have not forgotten all your training," Demona replied, pleased.

"How could I not have? This area was teeming with spells."

"It still is. Very few know about them and search them out. It has been our duty to guard and protect this magic, making sure that it doesn't get into the wrong hands. And it still is our duty. That is the spell you are searching for. But as you know, Tarwick is also hunting it."

"Himself?" Georgia asked.

"No." Demona pointed to the screen, and a line of magic flickered from her finger. The image changed to one of a blurred man. "This is who we believe to be Tarwick's spell hunter. We call him Z because no one knows his real name. He is incredibly illusive. You see we can't even get a picture of him."

"It's very blurry. That's a spell he's put on himself. So if anyone is looking for him, they won't know his identity." Smart, Georgia thought. If you wanted to last as a spell hunter, it was always best not to let anyone know who you were or what you looked like. Otherwise you might have nasty visitors showing up at your house trying to kill you—or recruit you.

"So," Georgia clarified. "We don't know what Tarwick looks like, and no one can get a clear picture of this Z."

"Correct," Demona said.

"I sense a theme."

Demona smirked. "You too, will want a glamour when you hunt, just like in the old days. Don't let anyone know your identity. That's what keeps you safe."

"Of course."

Demona pulled a vial filled with pink liquid from the air. "Here you go—instant glamour."

"Sweet." Georgia took the tube from Demona and studied it. The pink liquid was thick. When she tipped the vial, it slowly chugged its way from one side of the glass to the other. Since it was no larger than a test tube, Georgia slipped it into her pocket.

"The glass is unbreakable," Demona explained. "And you only need a sip."

"Will I look like my wildest dreams?" Georgia joked, pointing to the saddle bags that had taken over the backs of her thighs.

"You will look like...whatever it is you're thinking about," Demona said with a chuckle. "So be sure to have clear intent. And as we don't have very much of the potion and my potion-maker contact is currently on vacation, use it sparingly."

"Got it. What else?"

The witch clapped her hands. "You're to check in with me every night. Let me know your progress."

"How will I contact you?"

Demona winked. "You won't. I'll contact you. Any other questions?"

There was one, but Georgia was afraid to ask. She wanted to know how Diana was—where she was. If she'd ever recovered from that spell-hunting mission gone wrong. It was on the tip of her tongue. All the words had to do were to slip out.

"Yes?" Demona asked.

Georgia shook her head. "Never mind. I'll head out to the swamp right away."

"Good luck," Demona replied quietly. "I'm afraid you're going to need it."

CHAPTER 7

As soon as she was back in the minivan, Georgia called Hattie's son, Dow.

"How's your mother?" she asked after they had exchanged greetings.

"Not much change," he said sadly. "She's still in the ICU."

Georgia's heart cracked in two. "Will you be there a little later, in the early afternoon?"

"I will," he said. "I'm not going anywhere right now. Not until I know that my mother is okay."

"I'll stop by then, bring you some lunch. Do you like deli sandwiches?"

"I like 'em all," he said with a hint of amusement in his voice.

"See you then." They hung up, and Georgia pointed her minivan north, toward the swampy area that connected to the wildlife refuge.

A lake and its tributaries were part of the refuge. In the early spring, as it was now, plenty of fisherman liked to fish in the lake and the connecting streams and slower moving water, hoping to catch a catfish or even a smallmouth bass.

Today, as Georgia headed down a dirt and gravel road, there wasn't a fisherman in sight. Perfect. She parked her car under a tree next to a marshy area, magicked up a pair of waterproof boots and left the minivan, the mom-mobile of all mom-mobiles.

She headed into a forested area with very wet and mushy earth. This was the thing about spells, the sort that she hunted—they were visible to spell hunters. Invisible to the naked eye, yes, but Georgia could see them.

As she stepped into the forest and quietly made her way through the trees, she opened up the magic inside her. It bloomed like a flower, softening her to the power that existed all around the world—that which could only be seen when coaxed out.

And that's when it happened. Small orbs, ranging from the size of golf balls to tennis balls, appeared in the dim light that snaked between the trees. They floated like lint in a sunbeam, twirling and spinning as they bobbed up and down in the air. The spells themselves were magical enough to watch. But what they held inside, the power that could be unlocked, was a thousand times more special.

It was thought that the Native Americans, who had lived in the area before the settlers, had created the spells, and when the first settlers arrived, they added to the magic, making even more. But they didn't place the magic in locations that were easy to find. No, they had to place the spells in the stink-hole swampy area.

That was just like witches to make things hard for everyone else.

The spells themselves were all colors—crimson, cyan, magenta, gold, chartreuse, sienna—every color you could imagine. Each of the colors corresponded with a certain type of spell. But in order to know what spell it was, first you had to be able to read the orbs themselves.

Georgia could. Though none of the orbs looked like the mind-control spell she sought, she still took the time to read the magic around her. After all, you never knew when you might need a good laughing spell. There was nothing like a good laugh to make her feel better whenever she was down. So she plucked the forest-green spell that was, in fact, a laugh factory from the air and cursed.

She didn't have any way to carry it. But then Georgia smiled to herself. That was easy enough to fix. All she had to do was pull her old container from the magical place she'd stashed it—back at headquarters.

Demona's voice sounded in the air, nearly frightening the socks off Georgia. "You need your mason jar, don't you?"

"Don't do that," she said with a huff. "I'm at a certain age where I can have a heart attack, you know."

"Sorry. I should have thought. Here it is."

Georgia opened her palm, and a mason jar appeared in it. It was a regular-sized one, the kind that you'd use to store pickles or jam in. The only difference was that this particular jar had belonged to her grandmother and had a lace doily that fit snuggly around the middle.

It was a bit old lady-ish, but Georgia didn't care. She loved the history that the jar brought with it. When she was little, her grandmother would tell her stories of all the spells she had stored in it over the years, including the sneaky spells that seemed to have a life of their own and were almost impossible to catch.

Georgia unscrewed the lid and dropped the laughing spell inside. Then she magicked up a knapsack, stored the jar in it and slung the sack over her shoulder.

She had walked for several minutes into the marsh when she spotted a fisherman. He stood in the middle of the trees with waders strapped on—a waterproof rubber suit that looked like overalls.

He whistled while he fished, which was the first clue to Georgia that something was up. Any fisherman worth his or her salt knew that when you fished, you remained quiet.

His back was to her, so she couldn't get a good look at him. But a white-paneled van was parked across the road. The van itself wasn't suspicious. It had a picture of a key on it and a phone number for a locksmith. That must've been who the fisherman was.

But still something was off about him. He hadn't seen her yet, or so she believed. Georgia quietly made her way toward him.

That was when the van rocked from side to side. Someone was in there.

Now the fine hairs on the back of her neck soldiered to attention.

There were two choices—creep back the way she had come or confront the "fisherman." Seeing as how she hadn't used her magic in a while, bothering this guy might be fun.

Now why would a fisherman who worked for a locksmith be out in the middle of the boonies, and why would his van be rocking from side to side?

It wouldn't unless someone was trapped in it.

He probably had a hostage—some girl he'd picked up. That girl more than likely needed rescuing. This was what Georgia needed, to make up for her missteps and her inability to help others—like Hattie, like Diana.

Georgia brushed a loose strand of hair from her forehead. Crap. She'd forgotten to put on her glamour. If this guy was a psycho like she thought, she'd better look as helpless as possible. Quietly she slipped the vial from her pocket, uncorked it and took a small sip, imagining herself to look completely harmless.

Half a second later it worked, but Georgia was not happy with what she wore—a miniskirt, black knee boots and a tube top. It was way too cold to be wearing this. Besides, she looked more like a hooker than a helpless sorority girl.

She would have to talk to Demona about the glamour potion.

She felt her face, because it wouldn't do for her to look like a forty-five-year-old prostitute stranded in the middle of a marshy swamp.

Unfortunately her face didn't feel any different, so she quietly magicked up a compact and viola! Her nose was small and upturned, her eyes a perfect almond shape. Her skin held a luster she hadn't seen in years, and the circles under her eyes were a thing of the past!

If she didn't look completely different, Georgia would have sipped this glamour potion every morning after getting out of bed.

Just as she was looking at herself, the fisherman spoke.

"Nice day to go fishing," he said over his shoulder.

Well, at least she had his attention. She snapped the compact closed and would have slipped it in her pocket, but the miniskirt didn't have any.

Figured.

"I'm lost," she said. "Can you tell me how to get out of here?"

"Sure." He pointed toward the road that he was parked on. "Just keep walking and you'll find the entrance. Your car break down or something? Maybe I can help you?"

Her gaze flickered from the van to him. "Um, yeah. But I'll be okay. I just need a way out. You fishing for catfish?" As she watched him, she noticed he had a bulge in his back pocket. It was suspiciously round.

"Yeah," he said. "Not having any luck."

He turned away from her, and Georgia used a trickle of magic to lift the object enough that she could make out what it was. Her magic, however, had a mind of its own. Instead of a trickle, a full line of power snaked into his pocket and yanked out the object.

The mason jar (for that's what had been hidden in his pocket) launched into the air, spinning. It plummeted back toward the ground, and that was when it stopped falling—at waist height.

Georgia and the fisherman locked gazes. Her magic had not stopped the jar's decent.

His had.

They stared at each other for a split second, and in hindsight, Georgia supposed that moment was long enough for both of them to ascertain that the other had magic.

It was also long enough for each of them to decide that they were not on the same team.

He threw a line of power at her, which Georgia dodged. She sent a line of bolts at him. Thank goodness for menopause. The magic came out like a rainstorm.

"You're searching for the mind-control spell," she stated.

He flung his arm out, dispelling her magic with one blast of his own. Impressive. "That's not your concern," he ground out.

She wouldn't back down so easily. Georgia took a step forward. It was close enough to discern that he was cloaked in magic from head to foot—a glamour, same as hers.

"It is my concern," she said, "because I'm looking for it, too."

"Brave of you to say."

He lifted his chin. Even though the man was wearing a glamour, he had straight shoulders and a lean physique. He was fit, whereas Georgia was a size 10 squeezed into a size 8 skirt and hooker heels.

He continued. "This is a dangerous business that you're in. We don't make friends. And we don't share prizes."

She scoffed. "You think I don't know that. Whoever you are—Z, I guess? I know the rules of this game. I've been playing before you were born."

He threw his head back and laughed. "Stay out of my way."

"Stay out of mine."

He pointed a finger at her. "You can have a free pass this time, but next time you wind up in the same territory that I'm in, I won't be so nice."

Who did this jerk think he was? King of the Swamp Lands? "Oh, you won't, will you? I'm not some novice witch. I know what I'm doing." Sort of, she thought. But it was best for him not to know that.

"Then go away, Witch." Z, for she was fairly certain that's who she had encountered, lifted a hand. A tornado shot from his palm.

She would not be enveloped in that. There was no telling where it would take her. Georgia lifted her own hand and aimed her magic to counter it, but the whirlwind was too fast.

As it scooped her up, she heard Z say, "Better luck next time, Witch."

His arrogance burned her. She sent a line of magic at him. It hit him in the leg, cutting him slightly. Z grunted and waved his hand from one side to the other, cutting off her view from him.

The next thing Georgia knew, she was back at her minivan. The glamour was fading, and she was slowly returning to look like her old self, middle-aged lady clothes included.

She huffed as she got inside the vehicle and slammed the door. Georgia gripped the steering wheel as a thousand thoughts ran through her mind.

First, she was ticked at herself for being taken unaware by him. It should have been in the back of her mind that this was Z. Who else would be out in the middle of a swamp attempting to fish where there probably weren't fish?

A psycho killer, that's who. His van had ticked that box in her head.

Secondly, she had learned that lesson good and hard—accept that whoever she encountered out in the field had magic. She also had to be on the defense, more so than she had been. Next time she would be ready to bind Z and continue her search.

But he was a formidable wizard. She would have to do better. As she cranked the engine, Georgia realized something. Z liked to hunt for spells during the day. That meant Georgia's best chance of finding the mind-control spell all by her lonesome would be at night.

It was a date, then.

CHAPTER 8

"I've got chicken club or Reuben," she said. "Which do you like better?"

Dow Williams smiled at Georgia's offerings. "Now that depends."

Not the response she'd expected. "On what?"

"On which one you like better."

Georgia laughed lightly. "To be honest, I like them both the same. I find the chicken club is a lighter version of the comfort food that the Reuben offers."

"Same here." Dow gazed at her flirtatiously. No man had looked at Georgia like that since—forever. "So which would you prefer? I'll take the one you don't want."

For some reason the look he had given her made Georgia want to take the more feminine sandwich instead of gorging herself on dark meat and sauerkraut.

"I'll take the club." She handed him the other bag and sat beside him. "How's your mom?"

"She still isn't awake, but her vitals are stabilized."

Relief flowed through Georgia's veins. "Oh, thank goodness. You don't know how relieved I am to hear that."

"You don't know how relieved I am that you were there to save her," he said, giving her that shy, flirty look again.

Georgia stared down at her sandwich. "Darn it, I forgot drinks."

Dow put down his sandwich and rose. "I've got it." He crossed to a vending machine. "What would you like, water, diet, Fanta?" he added, a joking lilt in his voice.

It was Georgia's turn to shy away bashfully. "I'll take water."

"Water it is."

The machined popped out two drinks, and Dow returned to the bench they were sitting on. They quietly ate their meals in the waiting room.

He spoke after a few minutes. "Really, you know that you saved my mother's life. If you hadn't been there—"

He didn't finish his sentence, and Georgia found herself taking his hand and squeezing it gently. "But I was there. That's what's important."

He smiled and nodded. Then his gaze dropped to stare at her hand. "Enough talk about sad things. Tell me about you."

Uneasiness hit Georgia at the way he stared at her. His gaze washed from her hand to her face, and he smiled in an open, available way.

Heat flushed her skin. She cleared her throat. "Well, I've got a five-year-old that's in kindergarten, and I'm married—have been married for ten years."

"He must be very lucky."

He didn't act like it, she thought. Ignoring Dow's obvious flirting, she continued, "What about you?"

Dow shook his head. "You haven't finished. All you've done is give me your resume. Surely there must be more to you."

"Oh, well, you know how it is. I had a great career until I married."

"And then you gave it up for a man, is that it?"

His words struck her. "Actually I gave it up for a chance at a family." But I'm getting it back now, she told herself.

His lips curved into a smile, and his eyes filled with intrigue. "I think there's much more to you, Georgia. Much more than you're telling."

She laughed uncomfortably as a male nurse walked in. "Mr. Williams?"

Dow's head snapped in his direction. "Yes?"

"Your mother is awake. She's asked to see you."

He rose and gestured for Georgia. "You too. You're coming with me. My mother will want to see you."

Georgia dropped her sandwich into her bag and rose.

"Only one visitor at a time," the nurse said.

Dow smiled at him. "Surely you can make room for one more. We won't stay long, and from what I can see, your ICU isn't very full. One extra person won't be in the way."

The nurse started to argue but then stopped. "Sure. Just this once."

Wow. Georgia looked at Dow with surprise. As they followed the nurse down the hall, she whispered to him, "Did you work some kind of voodoo on him to let us both come?"

He chuckled. It was a nice sound. "Hardly. I think he just saw reason."

When they reached Hattie's room, she was awake. It looked like tubes ran to just about every part of her body. Machines beeped and a blood pressure cuff inflated as they walked in.

"Darn thing," Hattie said. "I want to rip all this stuff out and go home. I'm feeling better, I told the doctor. They can let me out."

"Now, now," Dow said with a smile in his voice, "you have to do what the doctor says. You almost died."

Hattie pinned her searing gaze on Georgia. "And I have you to thank for saving me, if my memory serves me right."

Georgia shook her head. "I didn't save you. The doctors did. I just called the ambulance."

Hattie extended her hand, and Georgia took it. "You saved me. Don't let anyone tell you any differently."

The nurse reappeared. "Time's about up. Sorry, but we can't let you wear her out."

Dow nodded. "It's fine. We understand."

They left the room and walked into the hall. "I'm glad I was here when she woke up," Georgia said.

"Me too," Dow told her. "I'll keep you updated on her progress. Maybe we could have lunch again."

Georgia laughed uncomfortably. She wasn't the sort to have lunch with another man behind her husband's back. But Dow's statement took her off guard. She simply answered, "Have a good day. Keep me posted on how your mother's doing."

He smiled. With that, Georgia left, feeling guilty for something that she hadn't even done.

~

HER PHONE RANG AS SOON as she got into the minivan. Georgia didn't recognize the number, but it wasn't a spam call.

"Hello?"

"Georgia, this is Missy from the PTA."

Oh, she had forgotten all about the PTA. "Hey, Missy. I haven't contacted the farm about the petting zoo yet. Sorry, it's on my list."

"Actually, that's not why I'm calling."

"Oh, it isn't?" Were she and Missy about to become friends? Surely not.

"You signed up to volunteer in the library today. Mrs. Brown called and said that you haven't shown up."

Oh, crap. Georgia had forgotten all about that. "Oh no, I'm so sorry. I'll be right there."

She hung up and headed to the elementary school. By the time Georgia arrived, she'd missed her time to volunteer, but Mrs. Brown, horn-rimmed-glasses-wearing librarian, let her volunteer anyway.

It worked out good because by the time she finished shelving books where they belonged, school was officially over. So she went and picked up Judy from her classroom and headed home.

While Judy played with her toys, Georgia started supper and then called Claudia.

"So, a lot has happened since yesterday," she said.

Claudia scoffed. "You mean a lot as in you're back in Demona's fold?"

"How did you know?" she said, surprised.

"How could I not know? I'm your sister. Of course you were going to run straight to Demona once your powers came back. They did come back, I assume."

"They did. And they're a bit strange. Demona had to bind them up. They've been unruly thanks to menopause, but right now I've got them under control."

That was true. The dishes weren't rattling. Everything appeared smooth sailing.

"I suppose this means," Claudia started, "that you're going to be needing a babysitter."

"I'm going to try to keep my work to daytime hours."

"Right," her sister said skeptically. "Because that's how it always worked out in the past."

"Demona and I have an agreement. She expects me to work during the nondangerous daylight hours."

"Okay," Claudia said, not sounding very convinced. "But just so you're aware, I have bingo on Saturday nights at the church."

Georgia laughed. "Bingo? Have you turned into an old lady?"

"You'd be surprised how many eligible bachelors show up to play. Granted, they're about sixty. But plenty of them love a younger woman like myself."

Georgia laughed. Claudia was three years older than she was. The idea of dating a man close to sixty made Georgia feel old, very old.

"Anyway, let me know when you need a babysitter. I'll be happy to help."

"I'm not going to need a babysitter."

"Famous last words," her sister said before hanging up.

Georgia stood with the phone cradled against her chest. She would not need a babysitter. Spell hunting would not consume her life the same way that it had before.

It wouldn't. She was certain of that.

Georgia exhaled. It was time to make the dinner salad.

DANE WAS DISTRACTED when he got home. "How'd things go today with Brad?"

"Huh?" He sat in the mudroom, taking off his shoes. "With Brad?"

"Don't you have a presentation that you're working on?"

"Right. Yes. It's coming along."

He rose with a grimace. "You okay?" she asked.

"Yeah." He raked his strong fingers through his thick hair. "Stupidest thing. I ran my leg into a desk today. Wasn't watching where I was going and hurt myself."

"Is it bruised pretty bad?"

He smiled. It was the charming smile that she fell in love with ten years ago. His eyes twinkled, and the corners fanned in a way that made her melt.

"It's not too bad," he said in answer to her question.

"Well, come on then, handsome. Let's have some dinner."

Judy ran in. "Oh, it smells good in here. What're we having?"

"Pot roast," Georgia replied.

Judy made a face. "With yucky carrots?"

"With yucky carrots," Georgia said with a laugh. "Come on. Let's eat."

When they were finished and the dishes were clean and Judy put to bed, Georgia went into the bedroom. Dane was already in his pajama top and bottom. His long legs were stretched out in front of him, and his laptop was on his pelvis.

He closed it when she came. Georgia sat beside him and walked her fingers suggestively down his arm. "So...Judy's asleep. Want to have some 'us time'?"

Dane yawned. "I'm beat, darling. Maybe tomorrow night?"

It annoyed Georgia that her husband looked good enough to eat and that she couldn't do a darn thing about it. "Well, maybe tomorrow then," she said.

He gave her a wobbly smile. "Sorry, but I'm beat."

"It's okay. I'm gonna do a little reading before I come to bed. Want me to turn out your light?"

"No, I'll get it."

Georgia left Dane and headed into the den, which was sort of a TV room/office with built-in bookshelves that stored rows of books— mostly paperback novels that Georgia had read.

She hadn't heard from Demona yet and knew her call would happen at any time. To be honest, Georgia was somewhat relieved that Dane hadn't wanted to get physical. What if Demona had popped in while they were doing the nasty? That would not have been good for her marriage, even as hollow as it seemed to be right now.

"It's a good thing you're alone." Demona's head popped up in front of Georgia. Yes, just a floating head. "I had hoped you'd wait up for me."

"We need to decide on a time," Georgia said, "so that I know when to be alone."

"How about this time every night?" her floating head replied. "You can call or text me if it's not good."

"I don't have your number. I tore your card to shreds."

"That wasn't very nice of you," Demona admonished.

"To be fair, I didn't think that I'd be wanting my powers back."

"Well, I'll text you. How about that?"

"You have my number?" Georgia replied, surprised.

"I've told you before not to underestimate me. I have my ways. Now. What did you discover today?"

"I think I met Z."

Her eyelids flared. "Really? Was he as handsome as I fantasize that he is?"

Georgia bit back a laugh. "I don't know. He was using a glamour."

Worry filled Demona's voice. "Does he know what you look like?"

"No. I had on a glamour as well. I thought he was a perverted psycho killer."

"And instead you discovered he was only a spell hunter." Demona chuckled. "How amusing."

"It wasn't. We fought. We each know that the other is searching. This raises the stakes."

"Be careful," her old mentor said. "Don't let him know where you live. We don't know anything about Z."

"Other than he works for Tarwick?"

"That's what we believe, yes. Oh, there's something I've forgotten to tell you."

"What's that?" Georgia asked.

"Very soon, Saturn, Jupiter and the moon will be aligned in a way that hasn't occurred in over a thousand years."

"Right, I know. My daughter's school is having a Spring Fling that night."

"Well," Demona continued, "on that evening, spells that are worked will be amplified. Tarwick's plan, I surmise, is to garner as many mind-control spells as possible, so that on that night, the magic will be so amplified that—"

"That he'll be able to control a whole town, maybe a state. Get people to do what he wants. He could get people to hand over their money, their homes. He could take over an entire state," Georgia whispered.

Demona nodded. "Tarwick is dangerous. I've only given you a glimpse of his evil, but there is more for you to know."

Georgia's stomach twisted. She didn't like being caught unawares. "How much more?"

"I'll send over a file, and you can read it."

"When will I get that?"

Demona winked. "Right now is your answer."

Sure enough, a tablet apparated into view. Georgia took hold of it. "What do you want me to do when I'm finished with this?"

"Keep it. There may be more information that I have to send you."

With that, they ended the "call" and Demona disappeared. Since she wasn't tired, Georgia flipped on the tablet, settled into a chair and prepared herself to read about the wizard Tarwick.

CHAPTER 9

Tarwick's dossier was in Demona's own hand. Georgia heard her voice as she read what the witch had compiled on the wizard.

Tarwick is not only an ingenious wizard, he is most dangerous. His attempts at garnering spells indicates he has a godlike perception of himself.

The first time that he came on my radar was nearly five years ago, when he attempted to resurrect an entire graveyard of spirits. His intention was to create an army of the dead, one that would do his bidding.

His cemetery ruse might have worked if it hadn't been for the fact that several witches heard of his plan and stopped him. The fight was an all-out battle. The witches managed to stop Tarwick, but not without losing several of their comrades in the process.

Tarwick shows no remorse for killing others of his kind. The cemetery plan foiled, the wizard then looked to other ideas to put himself in dominion over humans—including possession of human's bodies so that he could reach his goals.

One of those goals, I believe, is political office. If Tarwick can wiggle his way into a leadership role, then he will have the power he needs to change policies, in effect changing the way that the world sees our kind.

Humans do not believe in us as we exist. That's what has kept us alive for so long. Remember, there are more of them than there are of us.

But if Tarwick got into office, it is most likely that he would encourage those in the supernatural world to turn against humans, break them to our wills.

Tarwick would, indeed, crush humanity as we know it.

That is why this wizard is searching for the beacon of all spells. Mind control would be dangerous in his hands.

We would all perish—not just humans, but supernaturals as well. His ego is so out of control that Tarwick believes if you are not on his side, then you are against him, and he will do whatever he can to make sure that you are put down, in your place or destroyed.

So you see, my dear Georgia, it is imperative that we stop this wizard from finding any spell that could help him achieve his goals. The future of our kind depends on it.

CHAPTER 10

*S*o the future of the world depended on a middle-aged PTA mom with a five-year-old and a husband who was more interested in sleeping than having any sexy time.

Great.

The world might actually be screwed.

But seeing as tomorrow was a new day, Georgia turned off the tablet and slipped it in between a couple of paperbacks on a bottom bookshelf—a place where Dane would never find it.

After that, she hauled herself upstairs and went to sleep.

THE NEXT DAY Georgia had to rethink her strategy for tracking down the mind-control spell.

Since she didn't exactly feel like going up against the wizard Z again today, and he had been in the swamp early, Georgia decided to busy herself with other duties until a little later, when she thought Z might be on his lunch break.

As she cooked up scrambled eggs, the doorbell rang. Judy ran to it and peeked through the glass. "It's uncle Brad!"

Georgia plated the eggs, wiped her hands and answered the front door. "Morning, Brad. Come on in. You're just in time for breakfast."

Brad gave her a goofy smile, which was his signature smile as far as Georgia was concerned. "Oh, wish I could eat, Georgia, but Patty made me a stack of pancakes and I gobbled them all down."

Judy gave Georgia a dirty look. "Why don't you make pancakes, Mama?"

"Because I have to get little kindergarteners off to school, and there isn't always time for that."

They walked into the kitchen, and Georgia poured Brad a cup of coffee. "How'd the presentation go?"

"Oh, it went great," Brad said. "That Dane, he always nails that stuff."

"I'm sure he does," she murmured, remembering how he had clapped his laptop shut last night and went to sleep with only a few words.

She handed Brad his coffee.

"Thanks."

"You're welcome." She poured a cup for herself just as Dane walked in.

"It smells amazing in here." He kissed Georgia on the forehead and greeted Brad. "You here for breakfast?"

"No, I was just telling Georgia that I've already eaten."

"Pancakes," Judy said sourly.

Georgia rolled her eyes. "Just eggs, bacon and biscuits this morning." Dane always wanted gravy for his biscuits, but the only days Georgia had time to make it was on the weekends. This was not the weekend.

"What? No gravy?" Brad blurted.

Georgia could have killed him. Brad might've been Dane's closest friend, but he had a penchant for being completely annoying. Not his fault, she supposed. But there were times when she wished that he would keep his mouth shut.

Like right now, for instance.

Dane came to her rescue. "No gravy, but that's okay. I like it with butter."

Brad chuckled. "Yeah, that's okay, too."

Dane sat at the table, and Brad took a spot beside him. Georgia sat on the other side of Dane. They plated up breakfast while Brad spoke.

"That presentation went well yesterday, but from what I hear, we'll have to stay late tonight. The client wants to talk to us."

Dane's gaze sharpened. "Tonight?"

Brad checked his phone. "You'll have an e-mail about it. Rose just sent it out."

Ah, the mysterious Rose, the new secretary, Georgia thought.

Brad continued. "You know how advertising goes. You're always at the beck and call of the client."

"Great," Dane grumbled. "Sorry, Georgia. I wanted to be home early."

Dane was always working late. Most of the time Georgia and Judy ate and she kept his plate warm for him. But since he'd missed his own party, Georgia had thought he would be better about coming home at an earlier hour.

However, this might be just fine. If Dane came home later, then she could do a little spell hunting when Z wasn't around.

"It's okay," she told her husband. "I understand completely."

And if she got home before Dane, he'd never even know that she had been out to begin with. She'd have to put in a call to Claudia for some babysitting time. Looked like her sister had been right all along. Georgia *would* need her help.

Brad checked his watch. "We've got to get going. It's your turn to drive us into work."

Dane shoved the last of the biscuit in his mouth and kissed Judy atop her head. "Have a great day at school, munchkin."

"You too, Daddy," Judy replied.

Georgia smiled and kissed Dane's lips. It was a hurried kiss without emotion. "See you tonight," she said.

Dane and Brad left, leaving her and Judy alone. "Finish up, pumpkin. Let's get you to school."

IT TURNED out that Claudia was more than happy to watch Judy that night. She would even make them dinner.

"Thank you; you're a lifesaver," Georgia said.

"I know I am," her sister remarked. "I'll pick her up from school if you want."

"That would be great. It gives me extra time to get out there and get myself all together."

After Georgia hung up the phone with her sister, she headed out to the Patch's Farm, where she was going to ask the farmer there about creating a petting zoo for the Spring Fling.

The farm was about forty minutes east of town, out in the middle of the boonies. When Georgia pulled up, she was met by the farmer's wife. It occurred to her that this woman was also a farmer but there was not a feminine of the word farmer—no *farmess* existed in Webster's Dictionary as far as Georgia knew.

Not that it mattered. She spoke to the woman, Mrs. Patch, who was more than happy to help out with the Spring Fling.

"We'd love to set up a petting zoo at the elementary school. We'll bring rabbits and goats. Those'll be the best since they'll be easy to transport."

"The goats won't get nervous?" Georgia asked.

"Nah," Mrs. Patch said, tugging on her overalls. She might not have been a *farmess,* but the woman certainly dressed like one in a flannel shirt and Liberty overalls made of blue jean material. Her face was also weathered and dry, like someone who spent most of their days under the blistering sun. "Those goats go for a drive with me and Mr. Patch every Sunday. They're used to riding in a truck. Just like dogs, they are."

"Well, the school appreciates it very much. I'll let the PTA know."

"When is the fling," Mrs. Patch asked.

"Soon." Georgia gave her the date and thanked Mrs. Patch.

As Georgia made her way back to the car, she saw what looked like faint twinkling lights in the distance. She smirked. Spells. Well, wasn't that interesting? Georgia might have to return another time and check them out.

The first thing that she did when she got inside her van was to call Missy and let her know they had secured the petting zoo.

Missy sounded more miffed than pleased. "Well, I'm impressed. I'm guessing they'll bring their own hay in case the animals poop?"

Oh, Georgia was prepared for that reply. "I was thinking we could set up outside. I'll rent some breakaway fencing that we can put up just for that night."

What problem could Missy have with that? Georgia was spending her own money and not the school's to give the kids a fun petting zoo. It was a brilliant idea. Everyone would love it.

"As long as you can get it all up, then we can do it. I don't have anyone else to spare to help you. All the other volunteers will be busy with other activities."

"I didn't expect any help."

Missy gave her a petulant laugh. "Let me know if anything changes. I look forward to the petting zoo."

Missy hung up, and anger burned through Georgia's veins like a river of fire. Oh, that woman was the worst! Georgia would make sure this was the best dang petting zoo that the elementary school had ever seen. It would become legendary, as far as Georgia was concerned.

As she headed back into town, her phone rang again. She didn't recognize the number. "Hello?"

"Georgia," a man said. "How are you?"

"Dow?"

"The one and only," he joked.

"I'm well," she replied in answer to his question. "How're you and how's your mom?"

"She's doing okay. Asked if you'd come and see her."

Georgia felt the guilt of obligation hit her. "Sure. I'll come visit. I can be there in less than an hour."

"See you then."

When she arrived at the hospital, Dow met her outside. "Visiting hours just closed for now. They'll restart in a bit. Would you like to grab a bite to eat before we can see my mother?"

Worry gnawed at her. Had Dow called her just to have lunch? Surely not. As he smiled at her, Georgia felt that his intentions were innocent.

"Lunch sounds great," she said.

"There's a place around the corner that we can walk to."

It was a greasy hamburger joint, which sounded fabulous to Georgia. She always watched her weight (go up, unfortunately) but couldn't deny herself a hamburger when given the chance.

They found a booth and ordered. She picked a burger topped with pimiento cheese.

He eyed her skeptically. "Think that'll be good?"

"Well," she said coyly, "it's either that or the burger with peanut butter and jelly. I think I made the right choice."

Dow laughed. There had indeed been a PB&J burger on the menu, and Georgia had been tempted to order it.

"Mother talked about you after you left yesterday," he told her.

"Oh?"

"She said you've been coming into the store for years. That she gives you cookies. I can see why she likes you."

The way he looked at her made heat flush up Georgia's neck. She didn't like it. It had not been her intention to have a flirty, uncomfortable lunch with this man.

She glanced out the window. "She does give me cookies."

"When she gets out, if you continue to visit her in the store, I'd like it if you kept me up-to-date on her."

"What do you mean?"

"Like if her health seems to be slipping, or if she appears off, anything that seems amiss to you. She doesn't always tell me when something's wrong."

"Parents don't like to admit to when they don't feel well," she mused.

"Exactly."

As they talked, the beginnings of a hot flash worked its way from Georgia's core all the way to her cheeks. She grabbed the glass of water in front of her and pressed it to her face.

"Is it hot in here or is it just me?"

"It's just you." It could have been taken lightly, but the suggestive, hungry tone in Dow's voice was unmistakable.

His words struck a chord in her.

That was when all heck broke loose.

Her power, which had been behaving so well, decided to act on its own. The lights above them started to flicker, and the silverware began jingling.

Dow sat back in his seat, staring at the nearby tables, at the clattering silverware. "Is the train coming?"

They were located near the tracks, but it wasn't the train making all the racket.

The other diners glanced around as napkins shivered on the tables, their plates clacked and even their purses shimmied.

Georgia rose. "Excuse me." She headed into the bathroom as the racket continued. Once inside, she locked the door, turned on the cold water and splashed it on her face.

"Calm down," she told herself. "There's nothing to get worked up over. Concentrate. Control it."

She saw the silverware and the dining room in her mind's eye. She pushed her power out of her and let it get tangled up in the napkins and purses and lights. It took a moment, but after a hard yank, Georgia pulled her magic back inside.

She turned off the faucet and exhaled. "I've got to do something about the bags under my eyes."

They were bad. She dried her hands and moved to go, but stepped wrong and twisted her knee.

She groaned. "I'm getting too old for this crap."

Georgia limped from the bathroom and made her way back to the booth. Dow rose. "You okay? You're limping."

"Just getting old, I guess."

They sat and he pointed to their food. "The burgers arrived."

"Thank goodness. I'm starving."

"Did you see what happened a few minutes ago? With the silverware and everything? A train didn't go by, but everything was shaking."

She shrugged. "Maybe it was an earthquake."

"Huh," he said, appearing to work it out in his head. "I'll have to check the news tonight and see if that's what it was."

"Probably." She lifted her burger in both hands. "Let's eat. I'm starving."

"Oh, before I forget—"

"Yes?"

"The police think they found the man who shot Mother."

This was news. "Good. I'm glad."

He passed her a card. "They want you to call them. They need you to identity the suspect. They've shown my mother pictures, but she can't quite remember what he looked like."

She took the card. "I'll call right after I see your mother."

Dow smiled. "Please do."

They finished lunch, and Georgia visited with Hattie, who seemed to be feeling much better. If she kept doing well, she said, the doctors told her that she could leave in the next couple of days.

Hattie thanked her for coming, and Georgia headed to her van and called the police. They did indeed want her to come in, and they wanted her to do so immediately.

Next stop, the Harvey Police Station.

CHAPTER 11

She called Dane on her way over. "Guess where I'm going?"

"Where?" He asked.

"Jail," she said cryptically.

He sputtered. "What?"

She almost laughed at his outburst. "They think they have Hattie's shooter."

"Do you want me to meet you there?" he asked. "I can come right now if you need me to."

"No, it's okay. I'll be fine." She was, however, touched by his concern. "I shouldn't be too long. Besides, it's not as if I'll be face-to-face with the guy."

The worry in his voice didn't disappear. "If you change your mind, call me. I can drop what I'm doing and come home."

"I thought you were busy with your presentation."

"I am, but that can always change. My family is important to me."

Dane hadn't pulled through when she had asked him to before, and now he wanted to come to her rescue? No, she could do this on her own, thank you very much.

"I'll let you know if I need anything."

"Okay, I love you, babe," he said.

"Love you too," she said listlessly.

The police station wasn't far from the hospital at all. It was nearly close enough to spit on. She arrived a couple minutes later and was shown to an observation room.

Within minutes, several suspects lined up in a lit room. She and two detectives stood in darkness. They had relayed that the suspects couldn't see Georgia. She had watched enough TV police procedurals to know that was the case.

When the suspects in the lineup faced her, she picked out Hattie's shooter immediately. "It's him. Number four."

"You sure?" the detective asked.

Georgia nodded. "Absolutely. No doubt about it."

The suspects left the platform that they'd been standing on and walked out. Georgia was escorted to the front of the station. The detective went to get her coat, leaving her by the front door.

That was when she saw him—the robber who shot Hattie. Shouldn't he have been locked up behind bars? Georgia and him weren't supposed to see each other. But here they were, staring one another down.

There wasn't an officer beside him, which seemed strange, wrong even. He wasn't handcuffed. Before she could move and alert someone, the criminal moved to her in a rush. He suddenly stood in front of her.

The sounds of the police station—printers churning out papers, the chug of the coffee machine—they all silenced. Even the images inside the station itself melted—the officers walking and talking, the walls, they blurred into blobs of white and black, losing all shape and form.

Magic, she realized. The robber was using magic.

"What do you want?" she said.

"Things are not what they seem."

He hissed foul breath into her face. His eyes were wide with the sort of madness that made her back break out into a sweat. Which meant she would also have under-boob sweat. Not the most appealing of places to collect moisture.

"Watch your back," he said.

"What are you talking about?"

"Your friends are not your friends."

Then he was gone to the other side of the room. His wrists were cuffed, and an officer stood beside him, an escort, Georgia realized.

The whole encounter had been an illusion, one that had unsettled her. As she stared at the robber, he glanced up at her and winked.

She shivered and an icky feeling webbed her entire body. Before it could be shaken off, the detective appeared with her coat and handed it to her.

As Georgia left the police station, she couldn't help but think about what the robber had told her. That her friends weren't who she thought. Did he mean Demona? Who else could it be? If that was the case, she and Demona needed to have a come-to-Jesus.

~

"Is she here?" Georgia asked Toad when she entered headquarters.

Toad hovered in front of her. "She's not. She stepped out for a while."

"I'll wait if you'll let me in."

Toad unlocked the interior door, and Georgia pushed her way inside. Toad followed her. His wings fluttered loudly as he swung around Georgia and perched on a table.

"Why're you upset?" he asked in a softy, tinny voice.

Georgia tapped her foot impatiently. "Because Demona is playing me."

"I don't think so. She hasn't said as much to me."

"She wouldn't tell you if she was. You know how that witch likes her secrets."

He frowned. "She tells me most things."

"Like what?"

Toad sat cross-legged on the table. He stretched his arms above his head and yawned. "If there's one thing about being sentinel at this place, it's that I never get a good night's rest. I could really use one. Can I use your shoulder as a pillow, Georgia?"

"No. And stop evading the question. What does Demona tell you?"

He tapped a hand in front of his yawning mouth. "Well, for one, that Diana wants to see you."

A shock wave worked its way up Georgia's spine. "Why? I thought Diana hated me."

"You have created quite the narrative for yourself. No. She doesn't hate you."

"She should."

Toad blinked at her, his emotions unreadable. "Why should Diana hate you?"

"Because I'm the person who made her like she is." Georgia couldn't stand looking at Toad anymore, staring into that face which was so quizzical, so without blame. "That's why she never sent for me."

"The attack that led to Diana's disability was never your fault."

"I should have been prepared."

"You were ambushed by several witches. No one saw it coming, not even Demona. Do you think she would have sent Diana there if that was the case?"

Georgia shook her head. She didn't like thinking about it, reliving what happened all those years ago. And she didn't want to see Diana. Because seeing her would bring it all back.

"You're being childish, you know," Toad informed her. "If Diana wants to see you, you should just go."

Georgia shook her head. "If Demona wants me to see her daughter, she'll tell me so herself." Deciding that she didn't, in fact, want to confront Demona at the moment, Georgia decided to leave. She also found herself itching for a little spell hunting. It would help her blow off steam. "When Demona comes in, tell her that I'd like to talk to her."

As she walked away from Toad, Georgia heard him reply, "Will do."

THE REST of the afternoon slipped by quickly. Before Georgia knew it, it was time to head out to the swamp to start spell hunting. But before she did, Georgia called her sister to make sure that she didn't need anything.

"Is everything under control?" Georgia asked.

"Oh yeah, I'm sitting in the pickup line. Some blonde is attempting to direct traffic, but she doesn't know what she's doing." Her sister huffed. "Is that wrong of me? To stereotype a blonde and say that she has no clue what she's doing?"

Claudia was talking about Mrs. PTA herself—Missy. "No. It's not wrong when the shoe fits. And in this case, it does. Every once in a while the PTA president helps out with the line, but she makes it worse."

"Amen to that," Claudia agreed. "Anyway. I've got this under control. Just go out and do what you do. But Georgia, don't get yourself hurt. I'd like my sister to come home in one piece—so would her family."

"Roger that," Georgia said.

She hung up and headed to the refuge. When she arrived, Georgia was pleased to see that there wasn't a van parked anywhere.

"Looks like I got here when Z isn't," she murmured to herself. "Perfect."

If there was one thing that Georgia liked, it was spell hunting solo. It gave her the opportunity to read the magical orbs in peace and quiet. The spells were hypnotic in the way that they bobbed and danced in the air.

Winter was fading, but daylight savings time still had a strong hold on the northern hemisphere. The sun was already sinking fast toward the horizon when Georgia stepped from her minivan.

She stared at a swarm of orbs. They lifted from the ground to bob in the air and then sank back down, disappearing until they emerged again. It was a crapshoot on whether or not she would find the mind-control spell, but hunting was hunting—whether you were after deer or spells. The person who harvested the prize kept at it, even when it looked pointless.

This was also what Georgia loved—the thrill of hunting. Sometimes the spells could be read as clues. Find the right clues and track them, and you'd uncover the magic you were searching for.

For instance, a precursor to a mind-control spell might be a focus spell. Find enough of those and there might be a trail to what she sought.

At least that was what Georgia hoped.

Time quickly got away from her. It was easy for that to happen in the swampy forest. From the sounds of the birds chattering to the buzzing of insects, Georgia found herself engrossed in the outdoors and realized that she had missed spell hunting more than she ever thought.

When she first gave it up, she had Dane to throw herself into and the newness of their marriage. It was so bright and shining, their love, and Georgia had busied herself creating their home and finding ways to help earn a little extra money. They didn't necessarily need the extra, but Georgia couldn't sit around the house all day.

There were times when she thought about her choice to give up her powers for Dane, but Georgia knew it had been the right decision. After all, she couldn't be a witch and remain married to a human, not without him discovering her powers. And humans and witches didn't mingle, everyone knew that. The other funny thing about witches was that unless one used their powers, it was easy for them to slip through the human world unnoticed.

That's why Georgia hadn't known what the robber was to begin with—that he'd had magic. But if he had magic, why had he allowed the police to capture him? The illusion that he'd placed into her mind had been powerful. If he was powerful enough to do that, surely he could leave his binds.

It didn't add up. But Georgia knew that Demona had answers. She just needed to get them out of the woman.

All these thoughts flickered like lightning bugs in Georgia's mind— coming and then going, being filed away for later.

But still the man's words bothered her, that things were not as they seemed. Did Demona really want the mind-control spell for herself? The witch was certainly vain, but she'd always worked on the right side of spell hunting—stopping the bad hunters from getting spells that could harm others. Had Georgia been set up by Demona? Had the whole robbery been a hoax?

No way. An innocent woman had almost died. There was no way that Demona would stoop that low just to get Georgia to return to work.

Or would she?

Georgia had long thought it was possible that Demona had received intelligence about the ambush that led to Diana's injuries. But Diana was Demona's daughter. Surely the witch wouldn't have done that to her.

Still, Demona was a bit of an enigma. You never quite knew what the woman wanted.

All these thoughts swirled around her head as the forest grew dark around her. The blackness closed in quickly, and the trees became thick pines. The marshiness of the refuge retreated, and Georgia found herself in the middle of a wood.

Even though it was dark, Georgia wasn't taking any chances of being uncovered. The work she did was covert. No one needed to know who another spell hunter was. She pulled the vial full of glamours from her knapsack and took a small sip, imagining herself to look like Julianna Hough. She figured, go big or go home. The glamour also disguised her voice as well. If a witch or wizard knew the sound of your voice and trapped it, it could be used against you magically—same as the power of knowing someone's name. There was power in a name. There was power in a voice. There was power in a face.

Darkness surrounded her, and Georgia slid a flashlight from her pocket. She was about to click it on when a voice took her by surprise.

"Don't move," he said. "If you do, it will be your last."

CHAPTER 12

*I*t was him—Z. Georgia recognized his attitude immediately. He was a fool to think she would back down. He might have been a powerful wizard, but she was just as powerful a witch.

He had taken her by surprise last time by sending her in a whirlwind back to her van. That wouldn't happen again.

"And if I *do* move?" she said.

"I've already told you," he said in a testy voice. "It will be your last. You don't heed warnings well, do you? I thought I explained this the last time we met."

She shuffled her weight from one hip to another. "I don't heed warnings from wizards who think they know everything."

"You're new to this. Trust me. You should listen."

"To you?" He stood behind her and she hadn't moved, but Georgia did not trust keeping her back to a wizard for long. "I'm turning around."

"I said not to move."

"Or what? You'll shoot me with magic? That's awfully brave of you."

"Turn around then," he ground out.

She did so slowly, with her hands raised so that he didn't fire magic into her back. When she had made a complete circle, Georgia eyed Z.

He stood in shadow, of course, and probably wore a disguise. His voice was the same though, low and gritty. He reminded her of when an actor put on the Batman costume in the movies and always deepened their voice. This too, was part of Z's disguise.

Even though she couldn't see his face, she could feel magic swirling around him. "Do you always wear glamours?"

"You know how this job is. Disguises work best. Looks like you're learning to make yours better. No more looking like a prostitute."

She scoffed. "I only did that because I thought you were a psycho who'd kidnapped a woman and had her in your van."

He laughed. "Hardly."

A lightbulb went off in her head. "You have a partner."

"That's none of your business. Look"—he lifted a hand, showing his palm in a threatening manner—"the sooner you give this up, the better. You won't find what you're looking for."

She sneered. "I wager that I'll find it before you do."

"We don't even know that we're searching for the same thing," he said with a scoff.

Z was annoyingly calm during the conversation. Georgia's nerves were bundled in her throat. Adrenaline rushed through her veins. It was fight-or-flight time for her. But this guy, he stood composed while threatening her with magic.

"I know who you are," she said. "You're who we call Z."

"Then you don't actually know anything about me at all."

One thing she knew—he was certainly good at ticking her off. "I also know that you're working for Tarwick."

He laughed at that. "I suggest you keep your theories to yourself. They could get you killed."

"I know how this game works," she spat out. "You don't scare me. Your threats do nothing but spur me on."

He chuckled harder. "You just walked in on the middle of this. I've been searching for the mind-control spell for weeks. What makes you think that you can just walk in here and take it?"

She took a step forward. He stiffened but didn't strike. "What makes me think that, is because I'm the best spell hunter around."

"I've never seen you before."

"Perhaps you haven't been looking in all the right places."

"Look," he said pointedly, "as there can't be two of us in this game, I suggest you go home and get out of this before you get hurt."

"Who's going to hurt me—you?"

"No one stands in my way," he ground out. The way the words hummed in the back of his throat before he spoke struck a chord in Georgia. Z was dangerous. He was lethal—that much was obvious.

And Georgia wanted to best him.

"Now, it's time for you to go home," he announced as if it was already preordained and decided.

"No."

Surprise filled his voice. "What?"

"I said no. I'm not going home. You can't make me."

"You sound like a child."

"No. I sound like an adult who knows what she wants." Before Z had a chance to act, Georgia blasted him with a small stripe of magic. He countered quickly, blocking the attack.

She darted to the right, heading deeper into the forest. But he was right on her heels, throwing magic at her.

A bolt hit her in the knee. Georgia went down, hitting the ground hard. She grunted as Z bore down on her.

She clapped her hands, and Georgia vanished, reappearing behind him. She hit him with a line of power, right in his back.

Z grunted and whirled. Just as he waved his hand and sent a bolt straight at her, Georgia opened a portal and stepped through it.

She landed at her minivan, far from where she had fought Z. Not wanting to know if he would catch up to her, she hopped inside and zoomed away.

The entire time, her knee ached where he had hit her with the spell.

"Well, one thing middle age is good for," she murmured aloud, "is that no one questions a few aches and pains."

When she got home, Claudia had just gotten Judy from the bath. Georgia's daughter was wrapped in a towel, her wet hair dripping on the robe.

"She's eaten and been cleaned," Claudia said, grabbing her purse. "We had a great time. Why're you limping?"

Georgia groaned. "Let's just say I stepped wrong."

Her sister eyed her skeptically. "Right. I'm sure you stepped wrong."

"In case you haven't noticed, I'm getting old."

Claudia brushed her fingers over the lines on her own face. "All of us are, honey."

"Mama, my hair's wet," Judy griped.

"Coming!" Georgia shrugged out of her jacket and rolled up her sleeves. "Let's get your hair dry."

"Bye," Claudia said. "Talk to you tomorrow."

Georgia spent the next ten minutes drying Judy's hair and getting her tucked into bed. By the time she was finished reading a bedtime story and eating supper, she was exhausted.

And Dane wasn't even home yet.

It wasn't a surprise. Whenever he said that he was going to be late, he meant *late*. But this was later than normal. It was almost nine o'clock. Where had the time gone? It hadn't seemed like she'd been in the refuge for the better part of five hours, but obviously she had been.

And she still hadn't found the spell—not even a trace of it.

Perhaps she was barking up the wrong tree, so to speak. Maybe the orb she sought wasn't there at all.

She heard the garage door open, and she headed into the kitchen as Dane walked in, messenger bag in hand.

"Late night," she said.

He forced a smile. "Yep, late night. We had a lot to go over, and then Rose had to make everyone copies of what we'd done."

A stab of jealousy worked its way down Georgia's spine. "Rose, huh?"

He nodded. "Yep. She comes to all the meetings."

"But she's new."

Her husband shucked off his coat. "She's new but learns fast."

Georgia needed to meet this Rose. In her mind she pictured a pert twenty-year-old with boobs up to her chin and a butt like a shelf.

Yes, Georgia was jealous. Mainly because her rack nearly hung to her navel and her butt was sagging. If if wasn't for Spanx, her butt would probably be level with the ground.

"Hungry?" Georgia asked.

"No." Dane shook his head. "I'm tired. Going straight to bed. After a shower," he added with a tired smile.

Dane walked ahead of her, and she noticed that he was holding his back funny. "You okay?" she asked. "Did you hurt your back?"

"Tweaked it at the gym. There's nothing like getting old, you know?"

She thought of her knee. "I know. I stepped wrong and hurt my knee."

"Is that why you're limping?" he asked.

"You noticed?"

"It's obvious." He flipped on the light and headed inside the bathroom. "Be out in a few."

As soon as Dane had disappeared behind the door, Georgia headed into the study to retrieve the tablet and call Demona.

She sat in the overstuffed desk chair, closed her eyes and concentrated on the witch.

Demona's bodiless head appeared a moment later. "I thought you'd never call. Tell me, what's new?"

"What's new," Georgia ground out, "is that I went to the police station today to identify the man who shot Hattie."

"The elderly woman who owns the clothing store?"

"That's the one." Georgia pressed her fingers to her temples. "What I discovered is that he's a wizard."

Demona's eyes narrowed. "I'm sorry?"

Georgia nodded. "He told me that everything is not as it seems."

"And what do you take that to mean?"

"I don't know, Demona. Maybe you can tell me."

Her eyes narrowed. "I hope you're not suggesting that I am somehow not being honest with you?"

"If the shoe fits…"

Demona stiffened. "Georgia, I have been nothing but honest with you. I have told you that we're searching for the mind-control spell. I have even suggested where to find it. What exactly is it you think that I'm not saying?"

"I'm not sure. Who Z is, maybe? Do you know who he is and you've just been keeping it a secret?"

"I don't know him," she insisted through ground teeth.

"Then why didn't you tell me that Diana wants to see me."

Her jaw dropped in surprise. The witch quickly recovered her composure. "Toad. He told you."

"Yes, he did."

"Well, for starters, I didn't think you wanted to see her."

Georgia scoffed. "I don't even know what kind of shape she's in. She's never asked for me before."

Demona scoffed. "You were so raw after the ambush and Diana was so hurt that it took months to heal her. Besides, you were getting married and you'd already given up your powers. You dropped them like a pair of dirty underwear." Her voice hardened. "Do I have to remind you that you didn't want to be one of us, Georgia? You didn't want to be a witch. You'd had enough of spell hunting, of all of it. You wanted to be human. So I let you. I didn't bother you. I let you go. You're as much a daughter to me as my own, but when I saw that you needed to be left all alone to grieve, I let you."

"You let me believe that Diana would never be the same."

"Because it was best for everyone," Demona yelled. "The amount of healing required to save her, like I said, took months. It was a slow process. If I told everyone she was fine and then she really wasn't…well, I wouldn't have been able to live with myself. I had to do what I thought necessary to save my child and to protect myself. Same as you. So don't you throw blame on me and tell me that what I did was selfish, because you acted just as selfishly when you gave up your powers and became a human."

A single tear fell down Georgia's cheek. "You could have told me about her. The other day, when you came to the party to get me to return."

Demona shook her head. "It wasn't my choice. It was Diana's."

Georgia exhaled and rubbed her eyes. The idea of seeing Diana after all these years made her gut twist. Still, Georgia was a grown-up and once you reached middle age, you realized that you simply didn't care about a lot of stuff in the same way as you did when you were younger.

"When does she want to see me?" Georgia asked.

"How does tomorrow sound?"

Horrible, Georgia thought. "It sounds great."

"Good," Demona said stiffly. "See you then."

CHAPTER 13

The next morning Georgia's knee still ached. She silently cursed Z under her breath as she rose and showered. By the time she had breakfast ready—grits, toast, and eggs—Dane was walking into the kitchen along with Judy.

"Smells good," Judy said as she marched to the table and climbed up a chair to sit. "Give me all of it!"

Georgia laughed at her daughter's exuberance. Dane planted a chaste kiss on Georgia's forehead as he walked stiffly to his chair and sat with a grimace.

"Boy, you really tweaked that back, huh?" she said.

He nodded. "Yeah. I'll have to be more careful about how I work out."

She chuckled. "That you will. Oh, I forgot to tell you that I saw Hattie yesterday."

"How is she?" He spooned grits onto his plate. "Still recovering?"

"Hopefully she'll be able to leave soon. That's what her son, Dow, says."

Dane quirked a brow. "He been spending a lot of time at the hospital?"

"Yeah." She remembered their meal and felt a stab of guilt. "I got there before visiting hours yesterday, so he actually took me to lunch."

"Lunch? And how was that?"

Now the guilt really hit her. "He's wounded. You know, his mom is hurt. He's feeling bad. Dow seems like a sad, lonely person without much going for him."

Of course all of that was a lie. The man wore expensive clothing and nice shoes. He had money and a clear interest in Georgia.

"It was innocent," she added.

"Mama, what does innocent mean?" Judy asked.

Georgia smiled. "It's what you are."

Judy nodded. "Yep, I'm innocent. I've even got innocent lightning bugs."

"What's that, honey?" Dane asked.

"I found lightning bugs at school and am hiding them in my locker."

Dane and Georgia exchanged a look and laughed. "It's not lightning bug season," her mother said.

Judy shrugged. "Well, I saw them."

Dane rose and tousled her hair. "What an imagination you've got on you, kid. Wish I'd been so imaginative when I was younger."

"Me too," Georgia concurred.

Dane rinsed off his plate and checked his watch. "Brad'll be here any minute." Sure enough, a horn honked outside. Dane shouldered his messenger bag. "Gotta go, ladies. I'll see you tonight."

"Will you be late?"

He winced. "I don't know."

"Well, don't forget, the Spring Fling is coming up. You can't be late Thursday night."

Then Dane was out the door without a kiss goodbye.

GEORGIA KNEW when she got married that every day would not be sunshine and roses, but she never expected to become two ships passing in the night.

It felt like Dane didn't care. That he wasn't invested in them. He spent more time at work than he did at home. Even on the weekends, when he *was* home, he seemed distracted, as if his mind was occupied elsewhere.

They needed to talk about it. That was the truth. Maybe the upcoming weekend they'd have a chance. But there was a lot to do between now and then—like the Spring Fling and finding every mind-control spell she could within a hundred mile radius, and stopping Tarwick from getting the spells before the planetary alignment.

Crap. Georgia was exhausted just thinking about it. But still, there was even more to do because Diana wanted to see her and Georgia had promised Demona that she would be at headquarters bright and early.

So after she dropped Judy off at school, Georgia headed over to the warehouse to see Diana.

"She's not here," Demona said when she entered. "My daughter decided not to come."

"Why not?" Georgia asked, her stomach twisting. Did Diana still blame her for what happened? "Did I do something?"

Demona flicked her hand. "She didn't give a reason."

Bull. That was total and utter crap, but Georgia didn't argue. Yes, she wanted to see Diana and ask forgiveness for leading her into the swarm of witches who attacked them.

Demona sat on the chaise and folded her arms. "Tell me what you've learned so far."

The pain in Georgia's knee flared. "That Z is strong as a son of a witch. We've met up twice and both times he's just about kicked my tush. I'm still no closer to finding the spells, either."

Demona motioned for her to sit on a chair. "You know, sometimes what you need is perspective. Perhaps the spells we seek aren't at the place where we thought. We know the refuge is full of magic, but perhaps we're on the wrong track."

Georgia considered this. If the mind-control spells were easy to find, then wouldn't Tarwick already have them? Perhaps she did need to reconsider her tactics. And then she remembered having seen lights in the back of the Patch farm. Maybe she would find the spell there. That was the thing about magical orbs. They were always in groups and clusters. There would be miles and miles without a single spell, and then suddenly you'd come up on a spot where thousands littered the night sky. That's when it was easiest to see them, after all—at night.

"Okay, so I have a new direction to go in," Georgia said.

"Good. How's your glamour potion holding up?"

Georgia pulled the vial from her pocket. She had about half left. "Z makes sure he's glamoured every time we come in contact."

Demona smiled. "Anonymity is the name of this game. You know that as well as I do. A spell hunter who is 'made' becomes a dead spell hunter. Nothing has changed in that regard. I'll order more potion, but it will be a while before I'll have it in hand. Use what you've got sparingly."

Georgia rose. "I guess I'll be out hunting, then."

"Good luck."

She'd moved to leave when Demona's voice stopped her. "And Georgia?"

"Yes?"

Demona gave her a motherly smile. "Don't take Diana's inability to show herself as any fault of your own, dear child. My daughter is haunted like you are by the events of that past. She has faced many demons and will come to you when she's ready."

All Georgia could do was nod. A sob knotted up her throat, threatening to come loose. She swallowed it down and headed outside. There was one person who could make her feel better—one and only one.

So when she got back in the minivan, Georgia called Claudia. "Want to grab some lunch in a bit?"

"It's about time you asked," her sister answered. "Tell me when and where. I'll be there."

The sisters met at a cozy downtown lunch site that served hot soup and the best orange rolls around. Orange rolls were like cinnamon rolls except they were brushed with this delicious and sticky honey-orange glaze. They were, to be honest, absolutely amazing.

But since every other bite that Georgia put into her mouth seemed to add on an extra pound, she killed any idea of eating extra calories.

Claudia oohed at the menu. "It's shrimp and grits for me."

Georgia envied her sister's ability to eat countless amounts of calories and not gain an ounce. Claudia was tall and thin, every middle-aged woman's dream. She worked out every morning and drank lemon water most of the day, which allowed her to splurge at lunch.

"It's soup for me," Georgia said. "I could use some warming up."

The women ordered, and once the waiter was gone, Claudia

propped her elbows on the table and laced her fingers together. "So. How's your newish career going?"

"It's fine," Georgia said. "There's another hunter out there—a man. I keep meeting up with him, and he keeps besting me."

"Sounds like your relationship is ripe with sexual tension," Claudia said with a laugh.

"I'm married," Georgia reminded her.

"To a man who can't even make it to his own birthday party. It's no wonder that you decided to go back into spell hunting. He's not showing you any attention. Dane's absorbed with his work, absorbed with himself. I don't know. Goodness knows I've been divorced twice, so I don't have a foot to stand on. But I will tell you that in my experience, when a man isn't paying attention to his wife, he's paying attention somewhere else."

Now Georgia felt miserable.

Claudia continued. "He had every opportunity to be on time last week, and he couldn't even do that."

"What are you saying?" Georgia asked.

Claudia shrugged. "I seriously doubt that Dane's spending all that extra time at the office."

Her stomach fell to the ground. "You think there's someone else?"

"I hope not. I really do. But maybe you should start watching him more carefully. See if he's acting weird, stranger than normal. Less attached. I don't want Dane to be cheating on you. But I don't want him *to be* cheating and you never know it until she shows up at your doorstep."

Georgia's stomach went from twisted to completely knotted. This was worse than she thought. For goodness' sake, her own sister thought that her husband was a philanderer. Or at least she thought the possibility existed.

Maybe it was time that Georgia paid a bit more attention to Dane's comings and goings. She also felt the need to investigate this Rose who had so suddenly come into his work and seemed to be at every late meeting.

What was she going to do? Follow him? That didn't seem reasonable. She had a spell to find before the planetary alignment. This was more important than Dane's fidelity.

What was she saying? Was it really? If she had been asked a week ago which was more important, she would have said Dane. But now, now with this whole Tarwick-might-try-to-enslave-humanity thing going on, it sort of took precedence over her marriage.

"You're conflicted, aren't you?" Claudia asked.

"No. Yes. Yes, I am very much," Georgia admitted. She glanced around to make sure no one was listening and then said, "You see, there's this massive thing that could happen if I don't find a certain spell by next Thursday night."

"Like, within a week?"

"Right. There's a really bad guy who's searching for a spell that will give him the ability to control lots of people's minds so that he can rule the town, if not the state, and maybe the country."

"Sounds bad."

Georgia nodded. "And now I'm adding Dane's possible wandering eye, or rather something else, to the list for me to worry about? I'm not sure I can fit it into my schedule."

"I could snoop for you," Claudia offered. "You're my sister and I want to make sure that you're taken care of."

Georgia shook her head. "No, I'll figure this one out. You do enough for me already." Deciding that the conversation had been on her long enough, she said, "So, what's going on with you. Are you dating anyone?"

Claudia suddenly beamed. "In fact, there is a new special someone in my life."

"You dog! Why haven't you told me before now?"

"Well, for one, every time I see you, we're either slicing you up and working a spell, or I'm babysitting my niece."

"Fair," Georgia complied. "So. Tell me about him. It's been how long since you dated a guy?"

"Well technically I have a date at least every other Friday, but it's easy to get a seventy-year-old to date you when you're fifty. But this guy, he's closer to our age."

The waitress brought their food, and Georgia waited until she was gone before continuing. "I want to know more."

"Well," Claudia said after swallowing a bite of shrimp and grits that looked so delicious it made Georgia wish she had ordered it, "he's got all his hair. He has nice eyes, a wonderful smile, and he brings me flowers."

Georgia's jaw dropped. "Marry him. Right now. I'll officiate the wedding. But seriously, Claud, he sounds great."

"He's so thoughtful," her sister gushed, "always asking about me and how I'm doing, and offering to bring things for me. The other night I was under the weather and didn't feel like going out, so you know what he did?"

"Lassoed the moon?"

"Close. He went to the pharmacy and brought me a sackful of remedies to make me feel better. He even bought the Puffs with lotion in them to soothe my nose."

"You hate those tissues."

"I know, but I wasn't going to tell him that. See? He's thoughtful."

"Then why didn't you bring Mr. Wonderful to Dane's party?"

Claudia picked at her shrimp. "Why would I have brought him to something when I knew he would only be meeting half of my favorite couple?"

Georgia's stomach soured. *"Half* of your favorite couple?"

Her sister shrugged. "I knew Dane wasn't going to show. He hasn't before. Why should he have bothered to change that?"

Georgia studied her sister. "What is it that you're saying?"

"Look." Claudia wiped her mouth with her napkin and settled it in her lap. "What I'm saying is that Dane doesn't seem to see you anymore. I think he loves you, but when was the last time he really made an effort? Georgia, he works late most nights, can't even attend his own party, and when the robber pulled out the gun and shot that poor old woman, where was your husband? Did he rush right on home when you told him what had happened?"

Georgia shook her head. "I went to the hospital with Hattie. I didn't even call him."

"That's what I'm saying." Claudia made a purr of sympathy in the back of her throat. "You could have been killed or shot and you didn't even call the one person that you should have."

Georgia suddenly felt numb from her head to her toes. "All I thought about was that I could have stopped what happened to Hattie. If I'd had my powers."

"Something you can't share with your husband." Claudia paused. "Look. I'm not saying that Dane's a bad guy. I love him. He's family. But you're my sister, and I need to be looking out for you. You were my family first, before him."

Georgia forced a smile. "You're right. We're family. To be honest, I have more important things to worry about than Dane right now. You know, the whole evil-wizard thing is really taking up a huge chunk of my time."

Claudia laughed. "I've got an idea how you may be able to find out a little about Dane."

Georgia perked up. "How's that?"

Claudia took another bite of her food. "After we finish this and have a couple of orange rolls, I'll tell you."

Georgia groaned. "Not the orange rolls. I'm on a diet."

"Nonsense. You've got too much stress in your life to be on a diet. Come on. Let's indulge."

And when the orange rolls arrived, Georgia did indulge. Breaking her diet turned out to be a sinful pleasure.

CHAPTER 14

The next morning, Georgia made sure that Dane was late getting up by turning off his alarm while he slept. He did oversleep, as she planned, but only by a solid ten minutes.

It would be enough time. She hurriedly made breakfast and got Judy dressed for school. So when Brad knocked on the door, Dane was still taking his shower, probably wondering how in the heck his alarm clock had somehow gotten disabled.

"Brad," she said, opening the door before he had a chance to knock, "so good to see you this morning. Can I get you some coffee?"

Brad eyed her with surprise. "Coffee? Sure. That sounds great."

They entered the kitchen, and Georgia poured him a cup. Judy jumped off her chair and rushed over.

"Uncle Brad," she shrieked, throwing her arms around him.

"Hey, kiddo! Give me a high five." He lifted his palm, and she slapped it hard. "Wow. You're strong."

"I know it," Judy said proudly.

Georgia bent over. "Judy, I need you to pick up the toys in your bedroom before school. Okay?"

"Aw, Mama," Judy pouted.

"Scoot," Georgia directed.

Judy scurried off, and Brad glanced around the kitchen nervously. "So, um, where's Dane?"

"Oh," Georgia said very innocently, "he woke up late. Just got in the shower."

Brad yanked his collar. "Really? Maybe I should wait in the car."

"Nonsense." Georgia slapped the cup of coffee in his hands. "You can talk to me. There's something I want to speak to you about."

"Well, wouldn't you rather Dane be here?"

"Not really."

It was a known fact that Georgia made Brad nervous. Either that or Brad was always nervous. He was simply one of those people who was absolutely uncomfortable in his skin. Which meant that he would sing like a canary if Georgia applied only a teensy bit of pressure.

Even now, sweat sprouted on his forehead. He was a Nervous Nelly if there ever was one. The thing was, Georgia didn't know exactly what it was about her that made Brad so uncomfortable. They'd known each other ten years, and he never, not once, took a moment to relax around her—not even when they had Brad and his wife over for summer barbecues.

"Dane has been spending a lot of time at the office," Georgia started.

"Oh, yeah, well"—he blew air between his lips in exasperation—"we had that one presentation and now we've got another one coming up. They're keeping us super busy."

"He was late for his own party last week."

"Don't I know it." Brad glanced toward the kitchen door. "It can't take him that long to shower, can it?"

"He likes to really soap up his body," Georgia told him.

"Well, in that case, maybe I'll wait in the car."

Brad moved to leave, but Georgia cut him off. "Brad, I want you to tell me right now if something is going on with my husband. We've known each other too long for you to keep secrets from me. You owe me as much loyalty as you owe Dane."

Brad chuckled uncomfortably. "Georgia, there aren't any secrets that I'm keeping. Dane's just doing the same thing that he's always done. He goes to work, stays late, and then comes home."

"Tell me about Rose."

"Rose?" Brad must've choked on his own saliva because he gasped.

"You think there's something going on between Dane and Rose? Georgia, you've got it all wrong. Trust me, there's no competition there."

Dane sauntered into the room. "No competition for what?"

Crap. Her plan to slowly drain Brad of every bit of information he knew had gone all wrong.

"You know," Brad replied, "just the competition that we face every day. That whole thing—the other ad agencies."

He shot her a knowing look, and Georgia played along. "Yep, Brad and I were just talking about your work."

Dane took a steel coffee thermos from the cupboard. "There's a lot of it. Looks like I've got to head out, hon. I don't have time for breakfast."

As Dane and Brad made their way toward the front door, Brad turned around and made a little locking motion with his hand at his mouth, suggesting that he wouldn't tell Dane what they had discussed.

To be honest, Georgia didn't care if he did, because if there was one thing she was certain of...

After Dane gave her a quick kiss and hugged Judy goodbye, she shut the door behind them. She knew Brad had been lying through his teeth.

Something was going on with Dane. Now she had to figure out what.

THERE WAS a PTA meeting that morning. Georgia debated skipping it, but since she was in charge of the petting zoo and the Spring Fling was coming up fast, she knew that making an appearance was necessary.

As usual, Missy held the groupie moms of the PTA in rapt suspense.

"Y'all, this year is going to be the best Spring Fling ever. Not only have we secured the balloon man to come and make animal balloons for the kids, but we also have a bouncy castle and even a dunking tank that Principal Brock has offered to sit in."

Missy gestured to Principal Brock, who smiled and waved.

Georgia was fairly certain that the only reason why the principal would subject himself to being dunked in cold water was a chance to please Missy.

One of the parents raised her hand. "I've got the fishing-for-prizes game all lined up."

Missy smiled, her pink lips splitting wide. "You are such a blessing. Thank you for working extra hard to make that happen." Her gaze turned snakelike on Georgia. "And I believe that Georgia has an update on the petting zoo."

All gazes turned on her, and Georgia felt a hot flash the likes of which she'd never experienced rage through her body. She fanned her face and rose, suddenly feeling very old and fat in this group of thirtysomething women who were only now beginning to dye their lustrous locks of hair.

Georgia's hair had reached that limp, sad stage. No matter what she did, it would never be long and luscious again.

"I have great news. Patch's Farm has agreed to sponsor a petting zoo. They will come and set up with rabbits and goats. They'll do so outside so that we don't have to worry about any animal accidents. I believe they will also have hay to put down."

Georgia waited for everyone to say that she was as awesome as Missy and that she'd done a good job, when one of the mother's, the same one who apparently rocked the fishing game, asked, "And what about the children with allergies?"

"What about them?"

The woman scoffed. "How will we protect them?"

"I don't know. Give them some Claritin before the fling?"

The women collectively gazed at the floor in distaste. What was Georgia supposed to do? If a child was allergic to barnyard animals, perhaps they shouldn't be petting them.

"Maybe," Missy said in a silky voice that Georgia wanted to strangle right out of her, "you could get gloves for the kids to wear."

All gazes flipped to Georgia. She stood there, unsure of exactly what had just happened. "You want me to get gloves for all the children? I'm sorry, but what's the point of a petting zoo if the kids can't feel the fur of the animal?"

Missy gave a small, uncomfortable laugh. "The point is that they get to spend time with the rabbits and goats. Some of our population doesn't have the opportunity. And I think," she gestured to the other moms of the PTA, "that to ensure the safety of all the children, you make sure that each child who requests them has gloves at their disposal."

"No." It felt so good for Georgia to say. "No, I won't do that."

The women made a collective gasp. Missy spoke. "I'm sorry?"

Georgia, fully emboldened by the hormones (or lack thereof) raging through her body, replied, "We announce there will be a petting zoo and tell the parents that if their child needs to wear gloves so that they won't break out into hives, then they should supply them. End of story."

The room went silent as all the mothers and even Principal Brock stared at Georgia. Though she felt emboldened, Georgia quickly realized her faux pas.

She had challenged the status quo, being Missy, President of the PTA. When Missy spoke, Georgia was supposed to quietly do as was requested. She was to bow her head and smile. If the parents wanted gloves because they were too irresponsible to take charge of their child's welfare, then by golly, Georgia was supposed to make sure that there would be gloves for the kids.

And as the crowd continued to stare at her in silence, Georgia quickly tried to figure out a way to bring them back to her. Because in that moment, she was enemy number one, an outlier and soon-to-be outcast of the PTA. Her list of friends would shrink. Everyone would know that she had, in fact, wanted to put their children *in danger*, for goodness' sake.

This was a battle that Georgia could not win. The sooner she admitted it, the better.

"Well," she said slowly, trying to figure out a way to make this work, "I suppose that I could find some children's disposable gloves somewhere."

Did those even exist? Could they be purchased on Amazon? If they couldn't, then Georgia knew they did not, in fact, exist at all.

"What kind of gloves?" Missy asked.

Georgia shrugged. "Latex?"

The crowd groaned.

"Okay!" She recovered quickly. "Not latex. The other kind. The not-latex kind."

The women exhaled a sigh of relief. All of them. Every single one.

Good night, the way they reacted, you would have thought that Georgia was intentionally trying to hurt their children.

She cleared her throat. "I will search for non-latex gloves for the kids. On Spring Fling night, you can count on me. I will ensure the safety of each and every child, making sure that if they need to keep their skin safe lest they experience an anaphylactic response to the goats and rabbits, that they can."

Georgia waited for something—applause, maybe. It had been quite possibly the best speech of her life. But instead of anyone cheering her on or even making her feel good about what she'd said, the mothers turned their attention back to Missy as the president continued with the meeting.

Georgia slumped back to her seat, trying to remember exactly why she had joined the PTA to begin with. Wasn't she too old for this high school crap?

As she pondered this, she remembered that there was something more important than dipping the kids' hands in protective rubber. It was that Patch's Farm had spells located on it. Of that, Georgia was certain.

As quietly as possible, she rose from her chair and headed out the back door. Well, she could kill two birds with one stone. Ask Mrs. Patch if she knew of any gloves for kids to protect them from the horrible rabbits, and ask if she could take a look around the farm, see if she could find one or two mind-control spells.

CHAPTER 15

$\mathcal{M}$rs. Patch did not have any suggestions in regards to gloves, but she was willing to allow Georgia to meander around the farm under the pretense that Georgia was thinking of becoming a farmer herself.

Oh, she wouldn't start with a large plot of land like the Patch family owned. She would begin small—like over there in that one far corner of the farm, small. For that was the place that Georgia had spied what she believed were spells.

The magic looked to come from a hollow that was past an enclosure that housed several bulls. Georgia made her way into a thick patch of forest, closed her eyes and waited for the magic to flare around her.

When she opened them, sure enough, Georgia spied orbs. Spells of all different colors hovered around her. She glanced over her shoulder to make sure that she wasn't being watched; then she headed deeper into the pines to keep from being seen.

The spells here were different than what she was used to seeing. They were more connected to nature. There were spells for fire making, for concocting a rainstorm, for calling on the little people of the forest.

Wait. Little people?

As much as Georgia was tempted to grab a little-people spell, it seemed like an idea ripe for disaster. All she needed was to get home and then suddenly her daughter would find the spell and there would be angry little people of the forest flying around her house, shooting arrows at them made from sharp blades of grass.

Nope. Not a good idea.

So she moved on.

If she had been searching for anything other than mind control, she would have been in heaven. The Patch farm was a treasure trove of magic. But she wasn't looking for anything but the one spell, so Georgia let the others go.

But still, where there was smoke, there might be fire. So she kept on, going deeper and deeper into the forest. The day started to slip away, until the sun was about at mid-level on the horizon.

That was when Georgia looked at her watch and gasped. It was past time to pick up Judy from school!

She ran from the forest. Her breath came in ragged heaps. Her knee that Z had injured killed. It would definitely need ice later.

She crashed through the forest and headed toward her minivan. When Georgia got inside, she tried to call the school, but there wasn't any cell reception out where she was.

Double crap.

She threw the van into drive and barreled down the uneven gravel road. It took fifteen minutes to reach the highway and get a cell signal.

The school had called her three times.

She called them right back. "Harvey Elementary. This is Missy."

Great. Now she'd have to explain her issue to Missy. She was the absolute last person on earth that Georgia wanted to talk to. Maybe she could ask for someone else.

"Georgia Nocturne, is that you?" Missy asked in a prissy voice.

Her stomach cramped. "Yes, it's me. How do you know?"

"That's what the caller ID says." Georgia had been foiled by caller ID of all things. "What can I help you with?"

"Well"—was there a way to say this without looking like the worst mother on the planet? She doubted it. Well, here went nothing. "Missy, I lost track of time and forgot to pick up my daughter, Judy. I'm on my way."

"Oh, that's okay, Georgia," Missy purred. "Your husband just arrived and picked her up. He was super nice. What's his name, again?"

Georgia hung up and called Dane.

"I'm sorry," she said as soon as he answered the phone.

"Honey, go change your clothes." Dane's voice was slightly muffled. He was obviously talking to Judy. "I'll get your snack in a minute." To Georgia, he said, "Are you okay? Did something happen?"

"No. Yes. I got distracted. I've been out searching for something."

"What do you mean, you got distracted?" His voice was hard now. It dropped to a whisper when he added, "Are you saying that you *forgot* about our daughter?"

Oh no, this was bad. "No, I'm not saying that. Of course I didn't forget about her. I just lost track of time, that's all."

"Lost track of time?" he said, exasperated. "How could you have lost track of time?"

She couldn't tell Dane the truth. Witches didn't exist in his world except as women with green skin who made appearances in fairy tales.

"I'm sorry," she said, thinking quickly. "I was out at the Patch Farm. We had a PTA meeting today, and I had to go there to discuss the petting zoo. Mrs. Patch insisted on taking me around the farm. Stupid me, I left my cell phone in the car, and by the time I realized that it was so late, it was past time to pick up Judy. I'm sorry. It was an accident."

He exhaled and his voice softened. "Well, as long as you're okay. Why don't you head on home? I'll start supper."

Her brows rose to peaks. "You will?" Since when did Dane cook except to throw meat on the grill?

He chuckled. "I will. It should be almost ready by the time you get home. Judy's starving. Does she always come home so hungry every day?"

Georgia laughed. "Yeah, it's part of being a kid. They eat a lot, are always hungry."

"She's already swiped a small bag of chips and ate the apple I gave her. I've got to get some food in her fast before she eats everything in the cupboard."

"Okay, well, I'll let you get to it and will see you soon."

They hung up and Georgia was relieved. She hated lying to Dane, but sometimes a little white lie was what a situation called for.

As she drove, Georgia worked out the problem of the spells. Okay, so the refuge hadn't panned out, but Z was always hunting there, which meant he, or whoever had hired him, believed it to be the best spot to find the mind control magic.

The Patch Farm, though fruitful when it came to finding orbs, didn't house the right kind of power.

So where did that leave Georgia?

Somewhere in the middle, she supposed.

It seemed like the best idea was to return to the refuge, but when? Z worked day and night. His intelligence must be telling him that was the place to find the spells. It was like searching for a single needle in a haystack—it seemed absolutely impossible.

And the planetary alignment was coming up. She would need to talk to Demona, see if she had any other ideas on where to search.

The idea of going back to headquarters made her spine stiffen. At some point Georgia would have to face her past and talk to Diana. She would have to.

And then there was Dane and her doubts about him. Perhaps she could broach that tonight. Maybe somehow talk to him, or better yet, search through his things and see if she could find a hint of what he was up to in all his late meetings.

Uh, just the thought of snooping made her cringe. Georgia had never had a reason before to rifle through her husband's private affairs. But Claudia had put a little tickle in the back of her mind, and now Georgia thought that maybe, just maybe, it would be best if she did peruse her husband's computer and phone.

But she had to get them away from him first.

As promised, when she arrived at the house, dinner was ready. Baked potatoes and macaroni and cheese—a true spread for a man who never cooked.

"Wow," she said as she draped her coat over a chair. "Smells amazing."

"Daddy cooked," Judy informed her as she ran to greet her mother. "He made my favorites."

Georgia shot Dane a smile as she hugged her little one. "He sure did."

Dane threw a kitchen towel over his shoulder and came over. He looked down at her with pure love in his eyes. "You can't ever say that I don't take care of my ladies."

She chuckled and kissed him. "Thank you for coming to both our rescues today."

He pulled her into a hug. "Anytime." When Dane released her, he rubbed his hands and said with gusto, "Now. Who's ready to eat?"

Judy's hand flew into the air. "Me! I am!"

"Then let's dig in."

"AND THEN THE macaroni monster ate the baked potato monster," Dane said dramatically.

Judy giggled and rolled back on her seat. "No, you're making it up, Daddy! There's no such thing as a potato monster!"

"But there is a macaroni monster?" Georgia questioned, eyebrow raised.

"Of course there is," Dane said. "There are macaroni monsters everywhere. And if you don't watch out"—he grabbed at Judy—"then he'll get you! Bwahahaha!"

Judy squealed and dived under the table. "He's not gonna get me."

Finished with her plate, Georgia rose. "Okay, you two. Let's not get anyone hurt. I don't want you bumping your head on the table, Judybug."

"I won't, Mama." She crawled out from underneath and stood up. "All finished."

"Take your plate to the counter. I'll clean up."

Dane rose and took his plate to the sink. "Judybug, want me to get your bath going?"

Georgia nearly fell over dead. Dane had made dinner and was now wanting to get Judy's bath going? Had he fallen and hit his head? Or perhaps he was guilty of something and felt the need to be overly considerate in order to make up for his guilty conscience.

It was possible.

"Bath, bath, bath," Judy sang as she ran into the bedroom, peeling off her clothes along the way.

Dane picked up her discarded top. "I hope this behavior doesn't say something about the future of our daughter."

Georgia scoffed. "Our child is not going to become a stripper, if that's what you're thinking."

He winked. "You took the words right out of my mouth."

She opened her hand to take the shirt, and Dane handed it over but closed his fingers around hers and pulled her into a hug. He glanced down at her, and warmth flooded Georgia's body.

"I love you," he whispered before kissing her.

"I love you, too," she murmured when they parted.

"Now. Let me go give our kiddo a bath."

"She needs her hair washed," Georgia told him.

Dane called back to her as he headed into the bathroom. "No problem."

The bathroom was located in their bedroom—the en suite bath. Georgia had approximately five to ten minutes before Dane finished playing with Judy and washing her hair.

It might not be enough time, but it would have to do.

Georgia quietly closed the bedroom door and headed to the kitchen, where Dane had left his laptop case in a chair. She slid the computer from the case, opened it and sat.

She knew his password. Dane had told her what it was ages ago. It was easy enough to get in. She opened his e-mails and started reading.

They were mostly about work with some sports peppered in for good measure. Lots of inner-office correspondence from Brad and even Rose, who Georgia still didn't like.

There was nothing in his e-mails that looked suspicious. Maybe he wasn't cheating after all.

Or maybe he had a different e-mail account, one where he put all his clandestine correspondence.

She pulled up a popular free e-mail service, but Dane didn't appear to have a saved log-in. Okay, that wasn't the way to go.

She nibbled her bottom lip. Time ticked away. Georgia probably only had about two or three more minutes before Dane appeared.

Where could it be?

Georgia pulled up another popular free e-mail site, but he still didn't have a log-in.

Perhaps, she considered, her witch hunt (no pun intended) was focused on the wrong person. It didn't look like Dane had anything to hide, which meant that he actually *didn't* have anything to hide.

"All right, finish up," she heard him call to Judy.

Crap. He was on his way out. Georgia was about to shut the laptop when a message dinged.

The subject read—WE'RE ON FOR TOMORROW NIGHT.

"Honey," Dane called.

Her heart pounded. She quickly scanned the message as his footsteps came toward the kitchen. He was almost there. A floorboard creaked and she knew that any second now he would be peeking his head inside the doorway.

"Where are you?" he asked. "You've got to see how wet I am. Honey?"

Dane entered the kitchen. Georgia turned away from the sink, where she had a dish in her hand, and laughed. His shirt was wet from collar to untucked tails.

She laughed. "Your daughter likes to splash."

"That she does. I just wanted you to see before I changed my shirt."

He left the kitchen, and Georgia returned to the dishes. The message that she had read infiltrated her thoughts. Tomorrow night Dane was meeting someone.

Georgia planned to be there.

CHAPTER 16

The next morning, all Georgia could think about was the message that she had seen. She did her best to shove it aside but knew that she would have to be present at the meeting place that Dane was supposed to be at that night.

Funny enough, it was out in the country at a restaurant that only served a buffet-style dinner.

She'd have to do her best to be undercover.

"I'm going to be late tonight," Dane told her.

No shock there, but Georgia kept a smile on her face as she handed him his coat. "Want me to keep a plate warm for you?"

"No. We'll eat at the office."

At the office. Right.

"No problem," she said.

He moved to kiss her, and Georgia gave him her cheek. "See you tonight."

"Don't wait up." He turned to Judy and gave her hair a tousle. "Have a great day at school."

"You too, Daddy."

Georgia's stomach soured. As soon as Dane was gone and she'd gotten Judy off to school, she called Claudia.

"You're right. He's cheating. He's meeting the bimbo tonight at a restaurant. I plan to be there."

"Do you need me to help you scout them out?" Claudia asked.

"No. I hate to ask because you've done me so many favors already, but can you watch Judy again?"

"Of course I can watch her. You don't need to feel bad, sis. This is a big deal that you're talking about. Your husband is running around. We need to catch that sucker. Obviously I will watch Judy."

"Thanks. They're not meeting until six, so you don't have to pick her up from school."

"Good. That means I can have an early dinner with my boyfriend."

Even though she felt like she wanted to vomit because of Dane, Georgia still managed a smile. "I can't wait to meet this mystery man."

"I can't wait for you to, either. You're gonna love him. I just know it."

"I bet. Listen, I need to go. I'm here at headquarters."

"Oooh," Claudia said in an ominous voice. "Headquarters. It sounds so official."

"Trying to stop a wizard is official business."

"I know it is. Keep us safe," her sister told her.

"I'll do my best."

Georgia parked the minivan and went inside. Demona was making eggs, of all things, in the kitchen.

"Care for some eggs?" she offered. "I also have toast."

Georgia waved away the offer. "I'm at a loss when it comes to hunting. I don't think the spell is in the refuge. We know there is tons of magic there, but not the right kind."

She lifted a brow. "And what makes you say this?"

"Because Z is also searching there, but he hasn't found anything." Georgia dropped her knapsack on the table. The mason jar inside clinked against the hard surface. "If that's not a sure enough signal, I don't know what is."

Demona placed her scrambled eggs atop a slice of buttered toast and sat to eat. She waved her hand, and a cup of coffee appeared in front of her. Georgia considered asking Demona why she hadn't simply magicked up her entire breakfast, not just the coffee, but kept her mouth closed.

"So," Demona said, "you think that because you've gone to the refuge twice and didn't find anything, added to the fact that Z keeps going and obviously is coming up short, means that the spell we're searching for isn't there."

"Right. Wouldn't he have it by now if it was?"

Demona smiled in a way that made Georgia's spine quiver. It was the sort of smile that suggested that Demona knew something Georgia didn't. Demona liked to pull out surprises when Georgia least expected it, revealing some token of info that Georgia would wish she'd had eons before.

She hated that smile of Demona's.

"Maybe," Demona said, "this spell is smarter than we think. Perhaps it's hiding deeper in the refuge than we imagined."

"Or maybe it's not there," Georgia said flatly. "Look, Z is a strong wizard. He's bested me twice."

"You?" Demona laughed. "You must be getting soft, Georgia. The old Georgia that I know would never have let a wizard like Z beat her at anything."

Georgia raked a slash of dark hair from her eyes. It would be time to dye it soon. The white skunk stripe of roots was growing larger. It really showed this morning when she looked in the mirror. This whole aging thing really stank.

But to Demona, she replied, "I have been out of the loop for a while, but that doesn't mean my instincts are gone. Look. We know Z is searching for the spell same as us. He's not finding it in the refuge. There must be another place to look."

Demona placed her fork on her plate and magicked a tablet from the air. "I just received new coordinates yesterday. There is another place nearby that is said to be ripe with magic. Now, what kind, I can't tell you."

Georgia groaned. "You mean it could be the angry type of magic, the stuff that doesn't want people poking around in it?"

"Exactly. Which is why I didn't immediately tell you about it." Demona pressed a few buttons on her tablet, and an image of a map flared to life above the screen. Georgia instantly recognized it as Harvey and the surrounding area. A red dot marked a patch of green, and Georgia stared at it.

"I hope I'm not walking into one of those old Native burial grounds."

Demona grimaced. "I hope not, too. Those can be nasty places full of traps."

"The last time I found myself searching for spells on sacred land, I wound up in a hole and some ghost or something was beating me with a stick."

It was well-known among spell hunters that sacred Native American burial grounds were as full of traps and tricks as an Egyptian pyramid housing the mummy of a pharaoh. Natives, especially dead ones, did not like folks coming in and stealing their magic.

"Get some tobacco to leave as a token," Demona instructed her. "In case you do find what you're looking for. That should help."

Georgia smirked. "I doubt it."

Demona ran her fingers through her lustrous hair. Seriously. How did that witch have the hair of a twenty-year-old? Not one bald spot in sight.

"I'll send you the coordinates," Demona said, tapping a few buttons on the tablet. "Now. Is there anything else?"

She hated to ask. It made Georgia feel like a broken record, but she felt that it had to be done. "Diana?" she said, hope filling her voice.

Demona shook her head. "She isn't feeling well today. Maybe tomorrow you can see her."

Her hopes crashed to the ground, but Georgia forced herself to smile. "Okay. Sure."

She told Demona goodbye and headed out. Toad stopped her in the antechamber. "Chin up, kid. Diana will come around. She can be a little wishy-washy. She wants to see you. I know she does. But she's afraid."

Georgia scoffed. "What? Is she afraid that she'll want to wring my neck when she sees me?"

Toad shook his head. "No. Nothing like that. Diana told me once before she was afraid to see you because she didn't want you to blame yourself any more than you already do."

Well if that didn't make her feel lousy, Georgia didn't know what would. Selfless Diana was thinking of Georgia's well-being. Georgia should have been thinking more about Diana's when she told her that they had to keep moving forward. That decision led them straight into the ambush.

Georgia smiled. "Thanks, Toad. You helped."

Not really, but Toad wasn't human and he didn't quite get human needs and feelings. But it still wouldn't do to make him feel bad.

"You're welcome, Georgia," he said with a big smile. "Have a good day."

"You too."

THE COORDINATES GEORGIA had received would take her near the restaurant Dane was going to that night. Rage like hot lava worked through her veins.

Seeing as how there was no point in going to the restaurant twice in one day, Georgia decided to search the area later, before she would be spying on her husband.

As she drove home from headquarters, her phone rang. It was Dow calling.

"Hey, Dow," she said.

"Georgia," he said in his velvety voice that probably convinced women to drop their panties in one fell swoop, "my mother's being released today. She was hoping to see you a little later."

"Sure. How is she?"

"Doing well. She has something to give you."

Georgia was flattered but uncomfortable taking anything from the woman. "That's very sweet, but she doesn't have to give me anything."

"Well, she wants to, and what Mother wants, Mother gets." The words in and of themselves were innocent enough, but the way Dow said them made a chill race down her spine.

She laughed uncomfortably. "Well, okay then. Give me your address and I'll meet you at the house. When's a good time?"

He told her, and Georgia spent the next couple of hours returning to her house and researching everything she could find about the tract of land that she would be hunting that night. While she did so, Georgia pulled her mason jar out of her knapsack and placed it on the desktop.

The laughing spell bobbed quietly in the glass, ricocheting from one side of the jar to the other. It reminded her of that really old Atari game with the paddles and the ball. The gamer had to keep the ball from slipping through the paddles, constantly hitting it to the wall and back.

Wow. Games had really come a long way.

And double wow, Georgia was ancient to have remembered such an antique game.

She turned her focus away from how incredibly old she was and felt and pinned her attention on the area of land she would hunt, looking through old witch archives about the land.

The tablet that Demona had given her held a world of information about the magical world. Since most of the facts were penned by witch archivists, it could be trusted. This was not some subjective periodical that might or might not have text backed by data.

What was in the tablet would have been verified.

She pulled up the map and tapped the area. Immediately a box filled with words popped up on the screen. Georgia read.

This area, though ripe with ancient spells, is home to guardian spirits who do not like their magic to be taken.

Just as Georgia thought. Going into this area would pit her against spirits who would not like the white woman running around trying to take their stuff.

More than likely, they'd already had enough stuff of theirs taken in life. She would have to take lots and lots of tobacco in order to be able to leave with even one spell.

"Why can't things just be easy?" she asked with a groan. "Why can't I just go in, find what I'm looking for and leave? Now I'll have to deal with some *Raiders of the Lost Ark* crap."

Another old reference that just made Georgia feel like she had earned the thousands of gray hairs sprouting from her scalp.

Since she couldn't control the spirits that would make her evening difficult, Georgia knew the only other option was to attempt to sweet-talk them.

So she headed off to the convenience store to buy a carton of cigarettes and some tubs of dipping snuff.

Because she didn't know which tobacco the spirits would like better, and it was best to be prepared for the night ahead.

CHAPTER 17

*B*ut before the night ahead occurred, Georgia still had to see Hattie and Dow.

She found Hattie's house easily enough. It was only fifteen minutes from her own. After all, Harvey wasn't a very big town.

Dow answered the door with a big smile and a hug—which Georgia had not expected. Before she could react, he pulled her into his arms, nearly knocking the breath from her.

Georgia sucked air, trying to fill her lungs back up, and when she did, she realized that Dow smelled really, really good.

Her back stiffened. She untangled herself from him.

He smiled warmly. "It's good to see you, Georgia. I'm so glad that you could make it."

She felt heady from his scent. Georgia shook it off and gave him her own smile. "Anything Hattie needs, I'm happy to help with."

"She just wants to see you." He led her inside the house, which was clean with sparse furnishings. There wasn't any clutter, which was good to see. She'd hate it if Hattie tripped and fell.

Hattie started to rise from the living room couch and winced. Georgia motioned for her to stay seated.

"Don't get up. I'll come to you." She leaned down and gave the woman a hug. "How're you feeling?"

"Oh, pretty good for an old woman who got shot," Hattie said the words sharply, but a spark filled her eyes. "I'll make it. Dow, will you bring us some tea?"

"Certainly." He left the room, and Hattie pointed to an envelope on the coffee table. "That's for you."

Georgia shook her head. "You don't have to give me anything."

"But I do. Take it. If you don't, I'll burn it."

Georgia opened the envelope. Hundred dollar bills had been stuffed inside. There was at least a thousand dollars' worth.

"I can't take this." The amount of money horrified her. "I didn't help you in order to get a reward."

Hattie frowned, deepening her wrinkles. They were rivulets that ran north to south on her cheeks and east to west on her forehead.

"I know you didn't help me for a reward, but you're getting one." She sniffed. "Like I said, if you don't want it, I'll burn it."

Well, that seemed stupid. Georgia grudgingly opened her palm. "Thank you. It's very kind of you to do that, but you don't have to."

Hattie smiled warmly. "Nonsense, dear. You deserve it. Now, where is my son and that tea?"

Dow appeared right on cue. "I'm here. Also grabbed some cookies."

Hattie glanced at Georgia conspiratorially. "The cookies are store bought, but they'll do."

She laughed. "I'm sure they're better than you think."

Dow handed her a glass of tea. "Here you go. Drink up."

"Thank you." Georgia sipped the tea. It was awfully sweet, almost strikingly so. "Hmmm. Very good," she told him so not to hurt his feelings.

Georgia placed the drink on the table. She blinked and looked up at Hattie, who was smiling. Dow was smiling.

But Georgia had the strangest feeling, as if time had suddenly shot forward. She shook her head but couldn't shake the discomfort.

She glanced at her watch and nothing had changed, not one thing. It was exactly the same time that it should have been.

"Are you all right?" Hattie asked.

Georgia touched her forehead. "Yes. I guess it must've been the sugar in the tea. I'm not used to drinking it so sweet."

Worry filled Dow's face. "I'm sorry. Did I make it too syrupy? I have a problem with that."

Georgia dismissed his concern with a wave. "It's not a big deal, really. But I need to get going."

"So soon?" Hattie asked. "You just got here."

"Yes, I'm sorry. I've got...something to do at the school. I totally forgot about it, and have to get there before I get into trouble with the PTA. You know how that goes," she said in a joking voice.

Hattie and Dow looked at her blankly. Clearly they had no idea what it was like to get into trouble with the PTA. Hmm. Well, anyhow, there was probably something for Georgia to do at home.

She rose and thanked Hattie again for the money, telling her once more that she didn't have to give her anything. Dow walked Georgia to the door. He placed a hand on her back. His touch didn't feel comforting. In fact, it felt possessive.

Georgia didn't like it.

"Thank you for the tea," she told him.

"Are you sure that you don't want to stay?"

"I'm sure. Keep me up-to-date on your mother." As soon as the words were out of her mouth, Georgia instantly regretted him. She was giving Dow a reason to keep in contact with her. It wasn't what she wanted. She hadn't liked his hand on her back, but for some reason the words to shut him down or to give him a hint that their time together was now over, didn't leave her mouth.

Curse her hospitable Southern upbringing. Georgia had been taught to be nice to everyone. What a pain the butt that was.

"Did the police have the right man?" he asked.

"Huh?"

"When you went down to the station to identify the person who had shot Mama. Was it him?"

She nodded. "Yes, it was. Haven't they called you, told you that I positively identified the robber?"

Dow scratched his full head of dark hair. "No, they sure didn't."

Georgia thought of the wizard and shivered. He must've gotten out, spelled the police into making him leave. Goose bumps washed down her flesh.

"Well, maybe they'll call," she said, not believing it.

"Maybe so."

She turned to go, but Dow grasped her arm. His hands were like fire, warming her straight through her clothes to her skin. Georgia wasn't sure if it was real or simply her imagination. She felt out of sorts from all the sugar in the tea.

"Georgia," he said.

"Yes?"

"Take care of yourself."

"You too."

As soon as she got into her minivan, Georgia fired up the engine. She sat for a moment, trying to shake off the wooziness that still fogged her brain. When she felt alert enough to drive, she put the vehicle in gear and glanced at Hattie's house.

Dow had retreated back inside, but the curtains were parted. Between Hattie and Dow, one of them was watching her. Georgia had a feeling she knew which one it was.

CHAPTER 18

Georgia couldn't see the spells from the road. She couldn't even make out one flicker of light from an orb.

She stood in the restaurant's parking lot. It was nearly suppertime, and folks were parking and heading inside to feast on a buffet full of fried chicken (she could smell the grease from outside), cornbread, butter beans, okra, pinto beans, and probably a blackberry cobbler and maybe even homemade ice cream.

It was a good thing that Georgia had eaten before she came, because the scents trickling through the air made her mouth water.

She headed toward the woods, glancing around the lot to see if Dane's car was parked anywhere. She didn't see it. Good. That meant there was time to do a little hunting before she surprised him.

Just the thought of Dane arriving with a woman made her chest burn with anger. A chilly band of fury wrapped around her heart. She did not look forward to what she would have to face and in fact, didn't want to face it at all.

She should leave. After she finished spell hunting, Georgia should pack up and go home, forget all about trying to uncover the truth. Maybe she would be happier not knowing.

What a crock. She wouldn't be happy until she knew exactly what was going on with her husband.

It had been a strange day—from the tea at Hattie's, to buying enough tobacco to ship overseas as contraband into another country, Georgia had endured enough.

Her nerves were frazzled. What she needed right now was to find the spell, give it to Demona and then confront Dane, who would hopefully be having a buddy night with Brad.

As if that would happen.

No, Georgia had a feeling her luck was about to run out. As she slipped toward the woods, she glanced around again, noting that more cars had filled the lot. She also spied a line truck, complete with cherry bucket. Two men stood beneath a power pole, looking up. They didn't watch as she reached the tree line and disappeared into the pines and oaks.

The woods were quiet. A few birds chirped as the sun slinked away. The horizon was splashed in pinks and oranges, with a brushstroke of emerald thrown in for good luck, she supposed.

As Georgia walked deeper into the forest, the magic started to appear.

If she had been asked if this particular forest of magic had a personality, her answer would have been shy. The orbs, which at first appeared transparent, slowly began to fill with colors—crimson and cotton candy, blue raspberry and lemon. Yes, they looked good enough to eat. Even though she'd eaten, now she was getting hungry.

Dane better not be up to anything, because she was starting to get *hangry*.

Hangry was not a good look on her.

The orbs flickered all around, swooping near as if they were living entities that were curious about her. They bunched up in front of her leg, sticking themselves to her as if she was a magnet.

"Now, now. I'm not interested in taking any of y'all home. I'm only looking for one type of spell."

The magic, seeming to have heard her, released themselves from her jeans and proceeded to float in the sky.

That could have been one of the booby traps, Georgia figured. If she had grabbed a big handful of the spells and tossed them into her mason jar, she wondered what sort of fate would have befallen her.

Would the spells have attacked?

She patted her knapsack, making sure the five cartons of cigarettes that she'd purchased were still inside.

They were. Good to know.

She continued on, reading spells as she went. There were lots of curious-looking magic orbs—spells for making a pot boil faster, spells for getting rid of lice, spells to call deer, but not the one she sought.

It was getting late, and Dane would be arriving at the restaurant soon. Georgia could come back the next day and hunt for spells again. But that didn't make her feel better. The mind-control orb had to be out here somewhere. But where?

Maybe it was just deeper inside this forest, hiding farther back among the trees. Well, there was one good thing, she thought as she headed back. Z either didn't know about this place, or he didn't think it was worth scouring.

Which, if she thought about it too much, did not make Georgia feel particularly good about her decision to roam the area. Perhaps he knew something that she didn't.

As she headed back the way she had come in, the orbs lit her path. The sunlight had disappeared, and the thick forest of pines and oaks seemed to soak up what was left of the sun's rays.

She looked around but couldn't see the lights of the restaurant up ahead. The thing about spell hunting was that it was easy to get lost in the spells, inside their beauty. Time would expand, or perhaps it shrank. It did something, that much Georgia was sure of, because she felt like she always lost track of time whenever she was surrounded by magical orbs.

It was a bit, she supposed, like all those alien abduction stories that she remembered hearing about as a child. A bright light appeared in front of a person and the next thing they knew it was five hours later and they had no recollection of what had happened in the last few hours.

That's what slipping among a forest of magic was like, too. It wasn't because Georgia was dazzled by their beauty. The magic was spellbinding, hooking in the hunter and warping reality.

But anyway, Georgia's reality might have been a little warped, but it wasn't so warped that there wasn't a restaurant up ahead. Any minute she should see the lights of the building.

But she still didn't.

The orbs themselves were beginning to grow farther and farther apart, so she had to be on the right track.

But it was when she heard his voice that Georgia knew without a doubt she was going the right way.

"And I thought that I'd lost you," Z said.

She saw his dark outline but couldn't make out his face. Georgia suddenly realized that she wasn't wearing a glamour. With everything going on with Dane, she had completely forgotten to put on a disguise to go hunting.

Wow. She was really distracted to have forgotten Spell Hunting 101 —always wear a disguise. Don't ever let another spell hunter know who you are.

But for once Georgia didn't care. Her husband was most likely cheating on her. She couldn't find the mind-control spell, and the planetary alignment was coming up fast. How bad could it be if Z knew who she was?

And then she realized—very, very, bad.

She had a child to watch out for, after all.

So Georgia, though she couldn't reach the potion to change her looks, spoke in a deep voice. "I didn't think you were smart enough to find this place."

He laughed. "Very funny. Saw you go in. I thought you'd be gone by now."

He saw her go in? The linemen! He'd been one of them. That made sense because the first time she ever encountered him, there had been someone else in his van—a partner, she figured. He had someone who helped him hunt.

Georgia used to have one of those. That's what Diana had been to her.

"You're not going to find what you're looking for back there," she told him.

"Oh no? I'm pretty sure that I know how to search for a spell. It's not my fault that you've given up so quickly."

Oh, that did it. She had enough on her plate without having to deal with a smart aleck of a nemesis.

Georgia placed a hand on her hip in defiance. Not that he could see, but it didn't matter. "Go ahead and look for it. You'll be wasting your time. While you're off hunting for the wrong spells, I'll be finding the real deal."

"So you think."

"So I know." They both stood there, neither of them moving. Georgia found that her face was getting hot, which meant her blood pressure was on the rise. She didn't have time for Z's crap. She had to intercept her husband and his not-so-secret rendezvous. She felt like rumbling, and if Z wanted to, she was all for it. "Listen, you might think you're some hotshot spell hunter because we're in the middle of a forest that's across the street from a cornfield, but you don't impress me. I was spell hunting before you were even born."

She'd never heard of this Z before she retired, which meant he could've been a good twenty years younger than her.

Man, did that make her feel old. She had been born in the seventies and remembered thinking it was weird when kids were born in the eighties. But now babies were born twenty years into the new millennium.

It was unfathomable that she had gotten so old.

All she knew was that Z worked for the opposition. He was her enemy, and she was sick and tired of running into him day in and day out.

She started to move past him, but he shifted toward her. "I'm done with you. Stay out of my way, or next time I won't be so nice. I'll blow your butt to China. Well? Are you going to move?"

"We're on two different teams," he said, "going after the same prize. I think it's time we called—"

Whatever Z had been about to say, Georgia didn't hear it, because at that exact instant she took a step and the toe of her boot caught on a root, pitching her forward.

She yelled and Z, who must have been stupid, apparently thought that Georgia was attacking him. He threw out a line of magic that ripped into her shoulder.

She grunted and fell to the ground. Her knees smacked the earth hard, sending pain shimmying up her spine.

"That's it," she murmured. "I've had it with you."

She spotted a reveal spell that hovered in the air not far from her.

Georgia plucked it from the sky and threw it at Z with a whoosh of power.

The air shimmered around him, wrapping Z in a cocoon of light. He wore dark glasses, a mustache and had blond hair. Georgia watched as the light consumed him, grabbing the glamour that he wore and slowly dissolving it.

She rose and stared, glaring at him with a gaze full of spite. Finally she would know who Z was. It was stupid that they wore glamours anyway. Yes, it was for the spell hunter's safety, but Georgia didn't care about being safe—at least right now she didn't.

She was too angry, too fed up and too—just *too all of it* for her to have one inch of regret in grabbing hold of Z's glamour and yanking it from his body.

The light around him pulsed, almost as if it took a breath. Then it flared one last time, pulling Z's disguise away.

Darkness enveloped them, and Georgia opened her palm. An orb of light bloomed in her hand. It cast a warm glow on Z. Georgia, feeling very proud of herself, couldn't wait to rub into the wizard that she had bested him.

But when she lifted her gaze to meet his, Georgia gasped.

The man who stood in front of her, the man who had been Z, Georgia knew very well.

Her words ground out of her. "Dane, what are you doing here?"

CHAPTER 19

He scowled. "What am I doing here? What are you doing here, Georgia?"

They stared at each other, and the realization of what had just happened hit them each, hard.

Georgia was married to Z. He was a spell hunter working for the wrong team.

Dane wasn't cheating on her. Well, he might have been, but that wasn't what he'd been doing out here. He was looking for the spell to give to Tarwick.

Her mouth twisted in anger. "You're working with Tarwick? You've compromised me."

He threw up his arms in surrender. "I can explain!"

"No, you can't!"

Before Dane could say another word, Georgia hit him with a line of magic so bright it blinded him. He yelled in frustration, which gave Georgia time to escape.

She raced from the forest, finally seeing the restaurant's lights up ahead. She reached her minivan, threw open the door and started the engine.

She hit the road going close to fifty. A body ran out in front of her. She slammed on the brakes and pitched forward. Her breasts hit the steering wheel. What little bit she had was nearly crushed by the hard plastic.

"What the...?" Her gaze landed on who or what had darted out from the forest.

Dane.

They stared at one another, and Georgia hit the gas. Dane leaped out of her way, barely escaping being run over.

Georgia jabbed the phone button on the van's display and dialed her sister's number.

"Everything's under control here," Claudia said by way of hello.

"Get Judy out of there," Georgia commanded. "Now."

"Why?" Panic filled Claudia's voice. "Why should I get her out of here?"

"It's Dane."

"He's cheating? You caught him with the hussy?"

"Worse. He's a spell hunter."

Claudia sucked air. "You're joking."

"No." Georgia hit sixty-five to pass an old green truck going forty on the two-lane road she was driving on. "I'm not kidding. He's been a spell hunter all these years and never told me."

"Wow. He's really good at keeping secrets," Claudia said, obviously impressed. "I mean, y'all have been married ten years. And how ironic is that? You thought you were marrying a human, so you gave up your magic. He didn't."

"Don't remind me. I'm really ticked right now about that. But he's on the wrong side. We're working for different teams, Claudia. He's working for Tarwick."

"Oh," her sister said, realization sinking in. "That's the evil wizard, isn't it?"

"Yes, it is. Now that Dane knows who I am, that we're both after the same thing, he'll have to eliminate me. That's how it goes." The other line beeped. Georgia glanced at it. "Dane's trying to call."

"Have you considered that maybe he's not going to try to kill you?" Claudia asked.

"You're joking, right? He's working for Tarwick. I'm not going to allow him to have the spell, which means one of us has to go."

"I don't know," Claudia mused. "Surely you can find some sort of, like, agreement, don't you think?"

"Claudia?" Georgia ground out.

"Yes?"

"Just get Judy out of there. Get her gone, now."

"Will do. I'll take her to my house. You can come pick her up after you magically kill your husband. Pretty sure the government frowns upon that."

Georgia hung up before Claudia could talk any more smack. She glanced in the rearview mirror and saw two lights quickly approaching.

"Dane," she murmured.

The phone rang again. It was him. This time Georgia answered. "You know, I thought you were cheating."

"Cheating?" he said, sounding surprised. "Why would you think that?"

"Because you only kiss me on my forehead. You were late to your party—again."

"I told you that traffic was bad," he snarled.

"It wasn't bad. You were spell hunting," she said accusingly.

"See?" he said. "This is why it's stupid for hunters to keep our identities a secret. If I'd known you were a hunter—"

"I gave it up for you," she snapped, cutting him off.

"You did?" He sounded touched, and it annoyed her. "That was so sweet of you."

She barreled around a Ford Fiesta. Dane did the same in the utility van. "Where's your partner?"

"I left him."

"Him? Is it Brad? Is he a spell hunter, too?" Georgia accused.

"He helps me."

"Helps you work for evil wizards like Tarwick."

"Now, Georgia, you need to calm down. We can talk this out."

"Talk what out? You work for the evil side of the wizarding community. There's nothing to talk about."

"You've got it all wrong."

"Oh, do I?" she asked bitterly. "You never once told me that you were a wizard."

"You never told me that you were a witch," he threw back at her.

"You never asked!"

"Neither did you! And you'd better slow down because the speed limit is about to drop to forty-five."

He told her just as she passed the sign. Rather than thank him for warning her away from getting fined for going seventy, she pressed the red button on the dash, ending the call.

Georgia felt like she was crawling down the road toward her house. Dane was right behind her, and whenever she glanced in the rearview mirror, he was staring straight at her.

They reached the middle of town and were slowly approaching a green light. As soon as Georgia was underneath the light, she pointed her finger at it and made the light turn red.

Behind her, Dane's brakes screeched as he slammed to a stop. Her phone dinged a minute later.

You almost got me killed, he had written.

No, she thought. *I didn't almost then, but I will be almost getting you killed soon.*

She raced the rest of the way home, going as quickly as she dared. When Georgia pulled into the driveway, the house was dark.

Good. Claudia and Judy were gone. She parked in the garage and rushed inside.

Georgia kept the lights off and slipped from her boots, keeping her socks on. She padded quietly into the house, taking up position behind the kitchen island, using it as a shield.

These were the facts. Georgia and Dane worked for opposing spell hunting agencies. Knowing that he was employed by Tarwick meant that Dane was the enemy. He would kill her just as soon as Tarwick would.

And if Georgia found the mind-control spell before Dane? Then she was most certainly dead.

This—*this* was why spell hunters kept their identities a secret. But now both of their covers were blown, and it was all Georgia's fault.

She heard a vehicle door slam outside. A few moments later the front door opened slowly.

"Honey?" Dane said tentatively.

"If you leave now, I won't kill you," Georgia said.

He stopped. "Why would you kill me at all?"

She used a line of magic to throw her voice so that he wouldn't know where it was originating from. "Don't be stupid. We both know how this works. You work for the bad guys. I work for the good ones. Anybody finds out that we're spell hunters living together and we're dead anyway. Two spell hunters can't live under one roof."

"Who says?" he asked.

"We're not even supposed to know who each other are," Georgia reminded him. "Now, get out before I have to hurt you."

"You're my wife. You wouldn't hurt me. But do you mind telling me where our daughter is?"

"She's safe."

He took a few more steps. Dane was closing in. Georgia had been lied to, stood up and had felt like Dane had cheated, even though he hadn't. Georgia was done with him.

She had given up her magic for her husband, for Goddess's sake. Given up her job as a spell hunter. Granted, she had felt like she and magic were done after what happened to Diana. But Dane had lied to her for years—ten, to be exact. For how many of those had he been helping the bad guys? How long had he duped her into thinking that he was a good, decent human being, when the whole time he had been a wizard?

She peeked out from the island. Their eyes met. He lifted his hand, and before he could shoot, Georgia hit him in the knee with magic.

"That's for lying to me for the last ten years!"

He yelped and fell. A string of his own magic flew from his hand, narrowing missing her face.

She fumed. "You are trying to kill me!"

"No!" He waved his hand. "It was an accident!"

But before he could shoot and hit her, Georgia raced by, heading toward the stairs. She didn't want to go up and find herself cornered in a room, unable to escape. No, that wouldn't do at all.

Instead she tossed magic at Dane and raced behind the stairway wall, taking the time to catch her breath.

"Georgia, will you listen to me?"

"Why? It's all lies!"

"It's not all lies." He groaned and it sounded like he was getting up. "I'm not a healer, and I don't appreciate you hurting me."

"You hurt me first by lying to me every day of our marriage."

"Okay, let me explain."

She heard him pad toward her. Georgia whipped her head around the corner and threw a bolt at him. Dane ducked as her magic hit his computer. Sparks flew from the device. It had been properly destroyed.

Georgia couldn't help but smile.

"That was my work computer," he said, annoyed.

"Good. It'll be harder for you to get a message to Tarwick."

"I am not working for Tarwick! Will you listen to me?"

He started walking again, and Georgia sent another line of magic zipping straight toward him. He dodged the bolt before it clipped his gonads.

"Leave my male parts alone," he shouted.

"Your male parts deserve it," she yelled. "I thought you were cheating, but it turns out you're just a low-life wizard who's evil."

Just saying the words sent pain flaring in her chest. The betrayal ran so deep, like a cavernous wound that pierced her heart. A sob bubbled in the back of her throat. All she had wanted was a happy marriage, a happy family, but what Georgia had gotten were lies.

Angered again, she peeked out from behind the wall. Dane was nowhere to be seen.

"Where are you?" she whispered.

His voice came from behind her. "Right here."

She screamed in surprise before whirling around. Dane reached for her, but Georgia zapped him in the shoulder.

As she ran, she heard him yell behind her, "Dang it, Georgia! Would you stop trying to kill me?"

"That was for standing me up at your own party," she shot back as she raced toward the office door. "I need to hit you about thirty more times before I feel better."

"Just please, let's talk like grown-ups," he called.

She stepped quietly inside the open door of the den. From where she stood, she could see the hallway. Dane would have to come down this way sooner or later. If he tried another trick like surprising her from behind, she'd hit him harder than she had before.

He groaned as he slowly padded toward her. She couldn't see him, but she could hear him loud and clear. "For the past ten years I've been working with a group that tries to stop magical attacks from happening. We've been fairly successful, and yes, I'm a spell hunter. It helps that we live in an area rich with spells. The night of our party, I received information that Tarwick is planning to—"

"Yeah, yeah, I know. Gather a cluster of mind-control spells and use the inherent magic of the planetary alignment to magnify the magic. He plans to control thousands of people, have them do his bidding."

"Precisely," Dane said. "I had to start looking that night. No one knows where Tarwick is."

"Or the spell, though I bet I could have found it if you hadn't kept sending me away," she snapped.

His voice was close. He must have been standing just off the hallway in the kitchen. "As far as I knew, *you* were an agent of Tarwick's looking for the spell."

She scoffed. "If you'd taken the time to ask me, you would've known that wasn't the truth."

"You did the same to me," he countered. "You assumed that I was an agent of his. But I'm not. I never have been. And for what it's worth, I'm sorry about the party. I wanted to be there. I really did. But work…"

"Got in the way?"

He sounded sad when he admitted, "Yes, it did. But now you know the truth. We're both spell hunters. Wait. How long have you been a witch?"

A little of the old anger bubbled up in her. "I gave up my gift when we married. I thought that I was marrying a human. When you marry a human…"

Dane fell silent.

"Well?" she said, her heart hardening. "You just thought that you'd remain a wizard and I'd never know, didn't you? Just like a man—to have his cake and eat it, too."

He sighed. "I couldn't give up what I did. In fact, I'm surprised that we never met before."

What if they had? Images from the ambush that had hurt Diana flitted in her brain.

The words got clogged in Georgia's throat. They swirled with her emotions. "Maybe we have. Ten years ago, right before we married, I led another hunter to a field where we were supposed to retrieve a soft spell—one that can be manipulated into anything. We were supposed to be the only ones searching—"

"But you weren't," he said quietly. "We were told that a group was going to take the spell and use it for a portal that would tear the veil, allowing creatures into this world that shouldn't be here."

She gasped. "I was never told that. We never knew that. We were only supposed to retrieve the spell."

"You were set up." Dane stepped from the corner. Slashes of moonlight lit his face and body. She saw her husband as she hadn't seen him in years. He was fit, firm, with broad shoulders and a flat stomach.

Even in the dim light his dark eyes sparkled with intelligence. He ran strong fingers through his wavy locks and sighed.

"You were absolutely set up, Georgia. We were told that another group was searching for it to *use* it. I remember. There were two of you."

Cold dread washed through her. She had been set up? She and Diana had gone in, and for years Georgia believed that the ambush had been completely the work of the opposing side. But now it sounded like it wasn't an ambush that she had walked into, but an absolute set up.

Someone had gotten to Demona, told her the wrong information. Or had they?

Had Demona planned it from the beginning? Georgia's veins crackled from the fury working its way through her. She had been lied to about what happened all those years ago. Was it Dane, who now stood before her, or was it Demona, whom she had trusted for years—who had sent her own daughter into the line of fire?

Georgia shook her head. She knew who was lying.

It wasn't Demona.

Magic—menopausal magic, the stuff that was unruly, that didn't listen—flared on her fingertips.

"You're lying," she ground out. "And you've been lying for years."

Georgia lifted her hands and prepared to attack.

CHAPTER 20

She shot a line of magic straight at Dane's core. He raised his hand and created a shield.

"I'm not lying to you. Will you listen to me, Georgia?"

But Georgia was not interested in listening. She stalked forward. A look of absolute panic filled Dane's face. He pivoted on his heel and ran down the hallway and out of sight.

"I'm done being the nice PTA wife," Georgia announced. "I'm through with it. For all I know, you really have been cheating."

"What? I'm not cheating."

A shadow appeared from around the corner, and she threw a bolt at it. Georgia managed to shred the wall. Plaster fell to the floor in a crumbling heap.

"Well, now I know you're not cheating. You've been spell hunting," she snarled.

"Who has time for cheating when you're trying to stay in front of Tarwick?" he said.

"Who do you work for?" she demanded. "If it's not Tarwick, then who?"

She caught sight of Dane and blasted at him, hitting a cabinet and turning it into an explosion of splinters.

"I liked that cabinet," Dane yelled. "Stop destroying our house!"

"No, I won't. Not until you tell me."

"Okay," he said, his voice tense. "If I tell you, will you stop?"

"No." She blew up a map of the world that Dane had hung on the wall after they moved in. "I don't think so."

"Two can play at this game." Suddenly an object flew toward her. Georgia recognized it as a vase that they had gotten as a wedding present. She loved it because it was snowy white with a silver inlay of flowers that ran down the sides. She reached out to snatch it from the air when it exploded.

She yelled.

"Like I said," Dane told her, "two can play this game."

"I loved that vase!"

"Every time you destroy something of mine, I'll do the same to something of yours. Now. Do you want to talk?"

"About what?"

He ignored her question and launched right into what he had to say. "I work for an agency called Spell Hunters. We are hired to intervene when terrorist witches make plans. That's what we do."

"That's what I did," she told him.

"Who did you work for?"

"The company is called Magic Incorporated. We do the same thing."

"Doesn't it seem strange to you that two very similar companies wouldn't know about each other?"

She turned a corner quickly, hands ready to shoot magic, but Dane wasn't in sight. "No, it doesn't seem strange to me at all. Spell hunters are like tigers. We hunt alone."

"I have Brad."

She scoffed. "Oh yeah, and Rose. The new secretary. I forgot."

He chuckled. "You're not going to tell me that you're jealous of Rose?"

Georgia bristled. "Of course not."

"You are," he teased.

Where was he? She was going to kill him. "No, I'm not." She was. Georgia was most definitely jealous of Rose in the short skirts that she imagined the secretary wore. "I have more self-confidence than to be jealous of a harlot."

He laughed harder. "Wait until you meet Rose."

"What is so funny?"

"Just you wait."

As Georgia moved around the house, hunting her husband, it started to occur to her that he was Z. Z was a powerful wizard. Every time that she'd encountered him before, he had made short work of her.

But now her husband hadn't stepped out and defeated her. Why? What was he waiting for?

"We need to be working together," he told her.

"I don't trust you," she said.

Dane's voice saddened. "You've been married to me for ten years and now you don't trust me?"

He'd lied to her for years. "No."

"What's the name of the person you work under?" he asked.

"No names," she reminded him.

"I think we're past that now. We know who the other is. What we are. What we do," he said in a low, gruff voice. "You might as well confess."

Georgia didn't answer. He already knew too much. This couldn't end well. It would have to end, but it wouldn't be good.

She crept to the side of the dining room and placed her back to the wall that faced the hallway.

"Georgia?" he said.

He had whispered the word, but she felt the vibration through the plaster. Her husband stood on the other side of the wall. All she had to do was give it one good blast and all of this would be over.

She lifted her hands to do it…and stopped.

Dane whipped into the doorway, and before Georgia could argue, he took her face in his hands and kissed her long and deep. She started to sink into him as she inhaled the scent of his soap. Georgia wound her fingers through his hair, drinking deeply from his kiss.

Then she stopped.

That was when all hell broke loose.

She shoved him away and threw magic at him. Dane grabbed her bolt of power, plucked it from the air and tossed it across the room, where it destroyed a chair.

"I loved that dining room set," she yelled.

"Stop trying to kill me, and it won't be destroyed."

"No!"

They threw bolt after bolt at one another, making chairs explode, dishes blow up. When Georgia hit Dane with a hard line of magic, he dodged it. When he threw bolts at her, she shielded herself.

She had a bolt in her hand, ready to throw, when the doorbell rang.

"Oh crap." She stared down at herself. Her shirt was charred. Her pants had gaping holes.

Dane looked as bad.

"I'll get it," he told her.

Whistling, Dane went to the door and opened it. Two police officers stared back at him. One was bald; the other a brown-skinned, muscular man, pointed his attention at Dane and spoke.

"We received a call about a disturbance at this residence," he said. "Everything okay?"

Double crap, Georgia thought. Their situation looked like a serious domestic dispute. There was only one way to solve this before her and Dane's little war of the worlds got them into trouble.

She raced to the door. "Officers, I'm so sorry that we were too loud. Our child is spending the night out, and sometimes, we get a little…kinky."

Georgia put on what she hoped looked like a fairly embarrassed expression and slid her hand over Dane's back. He took her lead and hammed it up, shrugging and hanging his head. "Yeah. We get a little rough sometimes."

The officers exchanged a look before the dark-skinned man chuckled. "Do us a favor and keep it down, folks. People in the neighborhood are concerned."

Georgia saluted them. "Will do."

As soon as they were gone, Dane shut the door. They huddled by the window and watched as the cruiser drove off.

They exhaled a simultaneous sigh of relief. She sank against the door and ever so slowly lifted her gaze to meet Dane's. Love brimmed in his eyes. He cupped her chin in his hand and ran a thumb over her flesh. Goose bumps prickled down her spine. Though she was tempted to slap him away, Georgia allowed him this touch.

"Truce?" he asked.

It was the wrong thing to say.

She reared back and opened her hand. Magic flared in her palm. But as Georgia stared at Dane, emotion flooded her veins. Here stood the father of her child, the man she had given up her life for, and who, it turned out, would have accepted the witch in her without question.

They were fighting each other when they should have been combining forces.

Which was what her husband had tried to tell her, of course. But as she stared at him and emotion whirled within her, there was only one thing that Georgia wanted to do.

Jump him.

And she did. She launched herself at Dane, throwing her arms around his neck. Their lips met and they kissed deeper and longer than Georgia remembered them having kissed in years. He hoisted her legs up around him and grunted because, well, middle age.

Somehow Dane managed to avoid becoming victim to the minefield that was their house that evening. Plaster crunched under his feet, but he didn't slip and fall on broken glass. Within minutes he had Georgia on their bed and was slowly undressing her.

"I'm sorry that I never told you the truth," he murmured between kisses.

"You couldn't have. It's not allowed."

He nuzzled her neck. "I could have made an exception."

She giggled. "Yeah, right."

As they slipped under the covers, Georgia couldn't remember the last time that she'd felt so close to her husband.

It might have been never.

CHAPTER 21

Georgia's alarm woke her the next morning. She bolted out of bed and heard water running in the bathroom. Dane was taking a shower. Her body ached from the abuse it had taken last night, but she was also tingly, excited about the connection that she and Dane had made.

Her thoughts zipped from that to— "Judy!"

She scrambled from her bed to track down her cell phone. Last she remembered, it was still in her purse, which was probably in the kitchen.

The kitchen had been destroyed. Georgia couldn't help but giggle at the broken crockery and blasted walls. Well, it would take a lot of magic to fix all that. She wondered if Dane was up for it.

She found her phone easily enough and immediately dialed Claudia.

"Well? Is he dead?" her sister joked when she answered.

"Oh, thank goodness you're okay."

"Why wouldn't I be okay?"

Georgia paused. She actually had no answer for that. "I don't know. No reason. Of course you would be okay. It wasn't you who fought your husband to the death last night."

Claudia sighed. "Which makes me repeat my question—is your husband alive or did you kill him?"

Georgia laughed. "He's alive. Perfectly fine. The house, though, is another problem."

"Maybe you can use some magic and fix it."

"That's what I was thinking."

Claudia replied wistfully, "What I wouldn't give to be able to work a little magic in my life."

"Be glad that you can't," Georgia said. "It only winds up making trouble. My life should be case in point for that."

It was Claudia's turn to laugh. "I'm sure you'll figure it out. But anyway, your daughter is safe and sound."

"She's all right?"

"Of course she is," her sister replied stiffly. "I'm not a delinquent sibling. I can take care of a five-year-old. Want to talk to her?"

"Yes, and you don't mind taking her to school this morning?"

"No, I even grabbed her backpack on the way out the door last night."

"You are a saint," Georgia said, meaning it.

"I know. Here she is."

Judy came onto the line. "Mama, what are you doing?"

"I'm at home cooking breakfast."

Her daughter sounded miffed when she said, "Then why did Aunt Claud bring me to her house last night?"

"I was running late and wouldn't be home for a while. Did you have fun at Aunt Claud's?"

"We had fun. We had a sleepover, and I slept under a tent in the living room. You should come, Mama, and see my tent. You can sleep under it, too."

Georgia smiled. "I would love that."

Dane entered the kitchen, beaming at Georgia. He brushed his lips to her forehead, snaking a hand around her waist and squeezing gently.

"It's Judy," Georgia told him. "Want to talk to her?"

He nodded and took the phone. "Hey, Judybug. You having a good time?"

She couldn't hear her daughter's response, but while Dane spoke to her, Georgia made coffee and started scrambling eggs. She stepped over debris as she did so.

When Dane got off the phone a few minutes later, he wrapped his arms around Georgia's waist and gave her a long kiss.

"I missed you," he murmured.

"I missed you, too."

They stared at each other for a moment before Dane turned to peruse the kitchen. "This is a mess. What'd you say after breakfast we fix everything?"

She quirked a brow. "Is Brad on his way over to pick you up for work?"

"No." He gave her a pointed look. "You and I need to talk first."

"Oh?" She plated up the eggs that she had made and studied her husband. "What are we going to discuss?"

Dane pressed his back to the refrigerator and rubbed his thumb across his chin. "You and me—we work for different organizations. We've always worked for different companies. Doesn't that seem weird to you—that there would be two spell hunting companies in the same smallish city?"

He had mentioned that last night, but during their blissful encounter, she had forgotten all about it. She pushed a plate of eggs toward him. "You're saying that we're not working for two different people."

He ignored the plate of food. Georgia didn't know how. After last night's exercise, she was starving.

"Right," Dane told her. "I don't think we're working for two different places. I think one of us is being played."

"Me."

"You," he confirmed. "I hate to say it, but that's what makes sense. You were brought back into the world of magic. Why? Why now? You were also set up all those years ago. Also why?"

Georgia remembered the words that the criminal had spoken at the police station. He'd told her that all was not as it seemed. Her instinct had been that she couldn't trust Demona.

Had Demona set the whole thing up—the ambush years ago as well as Hattie's shooting? She hated to think so. It made Georgia's heart constrict to even consider that not only had Demona nearly killed her daughter, but that she'd also nearly killed an old woman.

But who else could be behind the strange coincidences?

Georgia looked up at Dane. He studied her, waiting for an answer. After a few seconds she nodded.

"Okay. After breakfast and after we clean up this mess, we go to headquarters—*my* headquarters—and get some answers."

Dane took a bite of eggs. "Sounds like a plan to me."

IT TOOK two hours for the two spell hunters to get the house in order. Lucky for Georgia, Dane knew how to work fixing magic like a pro. He even managed to mend the vase that she loved so much.

When he handed it to her, Georgia made a little purr of appreciation in the back of her throat. "Thank you."

"You're welcome."

His fingers brushed hers, and an electric jolt ran through Georgia's body. How she had ever thought that Dane was cheating was beyond her. It was strange though—sometimes it took breaking apart in order to bring two people together. For them, it took nearly destroying one another.

When everything was cleaned and tidied and Georgia had showered, they headed over to headquarters to confront Demona.

They took the minivan.

Toad gave one look to Dane and said, "No outsiders allowed, Georgia. You know the rules."

"The thing is, Toad," she said with a sneer, "I don't think he is an outsider. I think Demona knows my husband."

Toad froze. "This is an absolute breach of protocol. Demona will not tolerate it."

Georgia took a threatening step closer to the fairy. "If you don't let me in right now, I will pluck your wings off."

He gasped. "You wouldn't dare!"

"I would dare. Now. Let us in."

"Demona will have my head for this. Do you really want that? Do you want my death on your conscience?"

She cocked her head. "For some reason I don't think Demona will do that at all. I don't think she'll do anything bad to you. You're one of her cronies, Toad, and you and I both know that Demona takes care of her people. Now. Let us in."

Toad waved his hand. The door to the inner chamber appeared. "Don't blame me if she fries you both!"

Toad was still shouting when Georgia slammed the door shut behind them, drowning out his objections.

"Nice little guy," Dane said sarcastically.

"He usually is," she murmured, looking around. Demona was nowhere to be seen. "Demona! Demona, where are you? Come out right now!"

A far door opened. Georgia expected to see her boss, but it wasn't Demona who headed into the room.

It was Diana.

She looked as beautiful as the day that she had been nearly mortally wounded. Her long, dark hair shone, and caramel-colored skin glistened. She inhaled and stared at Georgia.

"Ah," Diana said quietly. "It seems the two of you have finally discovered one another's secrets."

"Diana," Georgia whispered. She had expected Diana to be hunched over, maybe walking with a cane, perhaps not even walking, but she looked perfect in every way. "Where's your mother? I need to speak with her."

Dane leaned over. "It's not her mother we need to speak with. It's her."

Georgia's gaze flickered from Dane to Diana, and then she understood. "You are over his company. You're my husband's boss?"

Diana crossed closer and gestured for them to sit.

Georgia shook her head. "I'm not sitting anywhere. Tell me what's going on."

Diana sat and smiled. "Something to drink?"

"No," Dane said. "We want the truth. All of it."

As Georgia stared at Diana, a knot formed in her throat. It was ten years of emotion, ten years of worry, ten years of regret, all of it charged up in her. For so long she had thought that Diana was barely alive, an invalid incapable of even the smallest of thoughts.

But here she stood—perfectly well.

Georgia lunged for the witch. She grabbed Diana by the hair and pulled. "I thought you were an invalid!"

Dane grabbed his wife's hand and, with the help of magic, untangled her from Diana. "Stop it. This isn't helping anything."

Diana smoothed her hair and dress. "You want answers. I have them."

"Start talking before I magic you off this planet," Georgia said.

Diana smirked. "You and I both know that you would need a spell orb for that kind of power."

"Try me," Georgia snapped.

Diana winced. "Okay. I'll tell you everything. Ten years ago you wanted to quit us, Georgia. You wanted out. You had met a man and were going to marry him. You were our best hunter. My mother didn't know what to do. She didn't want to lose you. So I stepped in, looking inexperienced. You took me under your wing and showed me the ropes. We thought that would be enough to keep you, but you still wanted to leave. You were going to marry some human, some man, and throw your powers away."

Georgia and Dane exchanged a look. A bad feeling overcame her, but she swallowed it down.

Diana continued. "So I hatched a plan to keep you. I thought if we created a second company and brought in more spell hunters, that would help. So we created a rival company, one that I led. Dane, it's good to see you here."

His jaw tightened. "I don't like being lied to."

Diana flicked her long hair over one shoulder. "I'm sure you don't. But I'm not the only one who's lied. Your wife never told you about her past. And you never told her the truth about yourself, either."

"You know that's not how it works," he snarled.

"Anyway." Diana stretched her legs in front of her and inhaled deeply. "I created the ambush. The mission that we were on that day, Georgia, it was all fake. It was made to look like I was nearly killed because of you. We thought that would make you stay, that you'd be convinced that it was your duty to remain with us. But you didn't."

Georgia lifted her hand. Diana nodded for her to speak. "So you're saying that you thought I would feel so guilty about what happened to you, that I would drop my fiancé and stay?"

Diana nodded.

"That is some sick logic," Georgia added. "Who does that?"

Diana didn't answer. "Mother healed me, and I continued my work with the hunters that I was training. You, Dane, you and your people. The company grew to something much bigger than my mother ever had. She retired, essentially. Until now."

"Until now," Georgia said. "Let me guess—the two of y'all thought it would be fun to pit husband against wife. Is that right?"

Diana shook her head. "No. We needed more boots on the ground in order to stop Tarwick. We needed you, Georgia. Don't you see that? I had to do everything in my power to keep you with us. Without your added help, we won't find the mind-control spell. Don't you see? We've done you a favor." She gestured to Dane. "You're working with your husband. With the two of you joining forces, you'll be able to find this spell and even more spells together. Just think—the two best spell hunters teaming up, searching out more magic than has ever been found before. With your gifts of sight, you can uncover spells that have been buried for years. We will find them, keep them safe so that the Tarwicks of the world will never be able to get their hands on them. Don't you see? I've done you a favor."

Her words struck Georgia hard. "A favor? Dane and I almost killed each other last night."

Diana shrugged as if it was no big deal. "But you didn't. You worked it out like the awesome spell hunters you are."

Dane exhaled hard. "Don't you think it would have been better if we'd known about one another?"

"You never would have believed it," Diana said matter-of-factly. "You never would have accepted it. You wouldn't have listened. No. This is knowledge that you each had to learn on your own. My mother and I couldn't have shared it with you."

Then the truth of it struck Georgia. "You never wanted us to find out about one another. You wanted to keep us separate. Your two best spell hunters joining forces? What could that mean for you? You wouldn't have control anymore." Georgia gripped the back of the red velvet couch in front of her. Her fingers dug into the soft cushion. The urge to rip it to shreds built in her, but she stopped herself. "That's what you want, isn't it, Diana? Control over us. You want us as your puppets, to go on this hunt or that one. You don't want us to actually think. You had years to let me know that you were okay, but you allowed me to believe that it was because of me that you'd been crippled. And look! You're not even damaged."

Dane smirked. "I don't know about that. She might be damaged on the inside."

"Good point. She could be, and probably is for thinking that it's okay to let your friend think that you're near death."

Diana chuckled uncomfortably. "Dane. Georgia. Let's just take a moment and calm down, shall we? Now we know the truth. Everything is out in the open. You're both spell hunters. You can both work for me now, stopping rogue witches and wizards from gaining access to spells that should remain hidden from them. Like now, for instance. You're both working together to find the mind-control spell. Dane, no offense, but you needed a little competition. You haven't been able to find the orb. And you, Georgia, your life was a sad, sad tale before you returned to us. For Goddess's sake, your job was at the bottom of a pyramid scheme."

Dane shot her a questioning look. "Was that clothing company a pyramid scheme?"

She cringed. "It might have been. I might have had to spend a little money some months to make sure that we stayed in a good position, so that I could continue to get commissions."

He rubbed his eyes. "You didn't have to work that job."

"No, I know. I mean, I stopped. It gave me something to do. My entire life can't be about dropping Judy off at school, going to PTA meetings and cooking you dinner."

He looked wounded. "You don't have to fix me dinner every night, babe. If you want to order out, we can."

She patted his shoulder to ease his mind. "It's not a big deal. I like cooking."

"Only if you're sure, and I can cook more from now on."

Diana clapped her hands. "Please. All of this is very touching, but do I need to remind you that we have bigger fish to fry? Tarwick is searching for the spell. If he finds it before the planetary alignment, we're going to be in deep trouble. All of us. So." She folded her arms. "I guess the question is, what do we do now? Georgia, I assume that you're going to join my company. And Dane, you'll remain with us, of course. Everything you've learned about spell hunting, you've gotten from us. It's a natural arrangement with the two of you. You'll stay and we'll become one big happy family."

Dane and Georgia exchanged a look. Dane spoke. "What do you think?"

Georgia pretended to consider it. "Wow. It is *so* tempting. You know, to stay with people who have lied to us the whole time that we've been working for them. She did nearly fake her own death. Gosh, what do we do?"

Diana's face reddened. "This is not a difficult decision."

"Oh, but it is," Georgia mused. "This is a toughie."

Dane rubbed his chin. "You know, I think we should quit."

Georgia gasped mockingly. "But whatever will we do? Where can we go without liars leading us?"

"Very funny," Diana said, annoyed.

Dane wrapped an arm over Georgia's shoulders. "I think we should work for ourselves. Start our own company. After all, there are a lot of people who want to keep spells out of the wrong hands."

"You wouldn't dare," Diana said. "We made you. We made both of you. You owe us."

Georgia smirked. "The only thing we owe you is that we don't let the door hit us on the way out."

With that, she and Dane left with Diana pleading for them to return.

CHAPTER 22

Dane called Brad after they left headquarters. Brad rushed right over and told them that he had given Diana his resignation as well.

The three of them spent the day going over ideas about what to do next, working over logistics. It wouldn't be easy for Georgia and Dane to start a new company, but it might work so long as Dane used his connections to reach out to those in the witch and wizarding government, the one that humans didn't know about. Dane had a reputation and at one time Georgia did, too.

"So you're going this alone?" Brad asked. "Are y'all sure about that?"

Georgia looked at Brad, and for once, he didn't appear so nervous that he was sweating. She wondered if that had been an act. If it was, it sure was a good one.

In reply to his question she said, "Dane really wants to. I'm still a little worried about it. It's scary not working for anyone else, to start our own company."

Dane pulled up a map of the area on his laptop. "We have a concentration of spells here. The problem is that we've searched all the major sites but still haven't managed to find what we're looking for. What are we missing?"

Georgia couldn't help but think dang, Dane looked handsome when he was working. How had she not noticed it before?

"What we're missing is that the spell isn't here." Brad scratched his head. "You and I have searched for weeks with no sign of it. We've covered every bit of territory. It just isn't here, Boss."

"But by all accounts it should be," her husband replied, folding his arms and sighing. "It's an old spell, one that the native people or early witch settlers would have created."

"I mean, if you could create a mind-control spell out of several different spells, then we'd be more on track," Brad murmured.

"But that's not how this spell works." Georgia rose and poured herself another cup of coffee. This was maybe her twelfth. "A spell that will force someone to bend to your will is created on its own. You can't use spare parts from other spells. You can combine lots of mind-taming spells and could, theoretically, control the entire world. But you can't take out a piece from one spell and sew it to another to get the same effect."

"Tarwick may have gotten the spell himself by now," Brad mused, "and nobody bothered to tell us."

"I don't think so," Dane said. "Someone would have reported it."

"Could be the whole thing's a lie," Brad added. "You know, to get you two together or to tear you apart. I don't know."

Georgia considered that. From the way Diana had acted, Georgia certainly wouldn't have put it past her to do such a thing, but something about that wasn't right in her mind.

She shook her head. "No. Tarwick's out there searching. We've got to find it. Even if he doesn't get the spell before the alignment, he'll continue to search."

"Then we may have to look outside our area," Dane said with a sigh. "There are plenty of other magical hotspots within several hours' drive. We can always spend a weekend hunting." He smiled, making the corners of his eyes fan. Georgia always loved it when his skin fanned. It made him look sexy. "And now I don't have to come up with a lame excuse that I have a conference just so I can get away. You can come with me."

"Yes, the years of lame excuses are over with." She winked at him.

"But maybe you could still do it every once in a while for old time's sake."

Brad lifted his hands. "Friends, we want to keep this meeting PG. No hanky-panky. At least I want to keep it that way. What the two of y'all do after I'm gone is up to you. But for now can we please keep the R out of this rating?"

Dane and Georgia laughed. "No problem," she said. "Brad, you want more coffee?"

He was about to answer when Judy's voice broke in. "Mama! Daddy!"

Their little girl rushed into the room and threw her arms around Georgia. "I missed you!"

Georgia pulled her daughter to her. "I missed you too, little girl. Did you have a good day at school?"

"Yes, my lightning bugs are really boinging. They boinged all day."

"What an imagination you have."

Georgia ruffled her hair as Claudia entered carrying Judy's back-pack. "I see everyone is alive and well," her sister said.

"We are," Dane answered. "And thanks for taking care of Judy." He gave his daughter a hug. "You don't know how much we appreciate it."

Claudia smiled wryly. "I love spending time with my niece. Children are so sweet at that age. In ten years I won't care for her, but right now I love her unconditionally."

Everyone laughed. Claudia turned her attention to Brad. "So. Are you one of them? A *hunter*?" she whispered.

Brad shook his head. "I wish. No, I'm more of an intelligence and logistics guy. I set things up, make sure Dane has backup, that kind of thing."

Claudia wiggled her fingers at him. "No powers?"

Brad shook his head. "My mother was a witch, but I didn't inherit that gene."

"Me neither," she said grumpily. "And Georgia here gave her power back to the goddess when she married Dane. Only got it back a couple of weeks ago. That was a fun ceremony."

"Oh yeah, I haven't told them all the gory details," Georgia admitted. "It was bloody, but don't worry," she said, noting Dane's pale face, "we didn't spill any on the tile."

"That's good to know," he said with relief. "I'd hate to think that another witch could come in and use that blood to hex you."

She waved him away. "Nothing to worry when it comes to that. But," she added, reining the conversation back in, "back to business. We only have a few days before the planetary alignment."

"We may have to work that night," Brad said to Dane. "To stay ahead of Tarwick."

Georgia scoffed. "There is no way we're working. We have the Spring Fling to attend."

Brad gave Dane a look that said, *Sure you do*. Georgia glared at Brad. "You are not about to come in here and tell my husband his schedule. He missed his own birthday party, for goodness' sake. He's not missing the Spring Fling."

Brad smirked. "Fine. But the two of you may have to leave early."

"We're not leaving early," she growled.

Claudia stepped in with a big smile. "I'll come, help you out with Judy in case you do have to leave. I'll even bring my new boyfriend."

Oh, to Georgia that sounded good after all. "You will? You'll let us meet him?"

Claudia rolled her eyes. "Only if everyone promises not to embarrass me."

"We promise," Judy said with a giggle.

Dane smiled widely. "Then it's settled. We'll go to the Spring Fling, and if Brad says he's got a lead, we'll leave to pursue it."

"In the meantime," I added, "we'll continue to search for the spell."

Brad pursed his lips but finally agreed. "Sounds like a plan."

CHAPTER 23

The night of the Spring Fling and the planetary alignment arrived sooner than Georgia expected. It seemed to her that she blinked and suddenly the day had come.

Or the night, she supposed. Dane was in charge of getting Judy to the fling. Which gave Georgia time to help set up the controversial petting zoo.

She had not managed to find child-sized disposable nitrile gloves. All she could find were the small size. She supposed that would have to do.

"Hey, Mr. and Mrs. Patch," she called as she approached the ring where the farming couple were setting up the goats and rabbits along with a bit of hay and some food and water bowls.

"Hello there, Georgia," Mrs. Patch said with her hands on her hips and a ready smile on her lips. "Good to see you again."

"Good to see you, too," Georgia replied. "Looks like it's almost time to start. Just a few more minutes. Is there anything that I can get you?"

Mr. Patch patted the front pocket of his overalls. "Nah. Got my dip in here, so I'm good," he said, referring to his chewing tobacco.

"Just let me know," she told Mrs. Patch. "I'm here to help with whatever I can."

Georgia moved to find Missy and check in with her, but Missy found her first.

"Georgia," the PTA president said with a huff. "It's about time you got here. I've been looking all over for you."

Oh no, what disaster could Missy possibly have to tell her about? "Everything okay?"

"Everything is not okay." Missy tugged her away from the farmers. "They are taking up entirely too much room. I also have to fit a cotton candy machine, a bouncy castle, and an ice cream truck into that space."

Georgia glanced onto the lawn, the "space" that Missy was talking about. A large swatch of grass spread out from where the petting zoo had been set up. There appeared to be plenty of room for everyone.

"I think it'll be fine," she told Missy.

Missy's face reddened. Clearly she did not like Georgia's answer. "And what about the gloves?"

Georgia pointed to the box she'd bought. "Right there. Plenty for the kids. Now, if you'll excuse me, I've got other things to help set up."

She left Missy and could practically feel the weight of her stare as Georgia walked off. A smile flitted on her lips as she entered the school to help put together the fishing game.

A COUPLE HOURS later and the sun had sunk below the horizon. It was barely six o'clock, and darkness already enveloped the land.

Georgia went outside to greet Dane and Judy. Cars were filling every available parking space and had spilled onto the grass. Kids were pulling parents toward the petting zoo, lining up to touch the animals.

None of them put on the gloves. Georgia smirked. Satisfaction felt good, indeed.

"Mama!" Judy ran up to her. She gave her daughter a hug as Dane approached.

Brad approached as well.

"Thought you'd get a taste of the Spring Fling?" Georgia joked.

"Very funny," Brad said. "My kid's are all grown up. You know that. Those days are long gone, and I'm happy about it."

"Want to show you the lightning bugs," Judy said.

"In just a minute," Georgia told her.

Dane glanced into the sky. "The planets are almost aligned. We missed our chance to find the mind-control spell. We can only hope that Tarwick didn't find it, either."

Sure enough, three bright planets were coming into a line. People were looking into the sky and staring before heading off to do the school activities.

"Hey, y'all. Meet my boyfriend."

Claudia had snuck up behind them. Georgia turned around, excited to see this mystery man of her sister's. But when her gaze landed on the beau, Georgia's mouth dropped.

"Dow?"

Dow smiled. "Georgia, good to see you. I've never been to a Spring Fling, but I'm excited about it."

Georgia gestured to Dane. "This is Dow. His mother is Hattie. The woman who was shot."

Dane's eyes widened in surprise. "Oh. Wow. How is she?"

"She's well thanks to your wife," Dow said warmly.

Georgia shot Claudia a confused look, and Claudia whispered, "We wanted to keep everything quiet, so we didn't tell you that we were seeing each other."

"Yeah, sorry for the surprise," Dow said. "We hope you won't be mad."

What in the world? Georgia wasn't mad; she was confused. Why would they have kept this a secret? His mother had been shot, for goodness' sake.

"Please don't be angry," Claudia said.

Worse, Dow had flirted with Georgia. He had, right? He had made comments and put his hand on her back. Now he was dating her sister. That was slimy.

Georgia forced a smile. "Let's get inside and see what projects the kids have been working on."

As they made their way into the elementary school, Claudia sidled up beside her. "I'm sorry that I didn't say anything. I thought about it at first, but then I wanted to make sure of how I felt for Dow and how he felt about me before I let you know who he was."

"You just said that both of you wanted to keep it quiet," Georgia said with bite.

"We did, but I also wanted to keep it on the down low. Sorry."

As they entered the school, Georgia waved her away. "It's fine. Whatever makes you happy. But Claudia, I don't know." Georgia was about to tell her sister that she thought Dow had been flirting with her, when Judy ran ahead of them.

"Come see my lightning bugs," she called.

"Looks like we have to see her pets," Claudia said.

Georgia smirked. "Right. She doesn't have lightning bugs. I wonder what she does have."

The group followed Judy into the classroom, which was chock-full of parents and kids. Kids were showing parents where they sat and their latest, greatest drawing. Judy rushed over to her locker and opened it.

She pulled out a small mason jar that she must've snagged from their house. "See? My lightning bugs."

Claudia squinted. "I don't see anything."

Georgia gasped. Inside the jar were at least half a dozen spells. It was impossible to count how many because of how jumbled all the orbs were. There wasn't room for them to move around.

Dane slowly approached Judy. "Can I see your bugs?"

"Sure, Daddy." She handed him the jar proudly. "See them? No one else can."

Dane shot Georgia a pointed look. "I sure can. I bet Mommy can, too. Come here, Georgia."

Georgia approached and gasped. There they were—the mind-control spells! A cluster of orange orbs must've existed on the playground or somewhere nearby for Judy to have grabbed them.

The spells had been under their noses this entire time, and Dane and Georgia hadn't known about them. Georgia reached for the glass.

"Judy, honey, is it okay if we take these home?"

Judy nodded. "Okay, Mommy. But you can't break the glass, and you have to take care of my bugs."

She patted her daughter's head. "I will, sweetheart. Don't you worry."

As Georgia was about to put the jar of spells into her pocket, Dow's hand shot out and grabbed her wrist.

"Thank you, but I'll be taking those."

Before Georgia could protest, he hit her with a spell that paralyzed her. She watched helplessly as he hit Dane, Brad and Claudia with the same magic.

Dow winked at them. "I knew you'd lead me to it. That should hold you just long enough for me to escape."

Dow started to walk off, but Judy yelled at him. "What'd you do to my mommy?" Her face went crimson, and Judy balled up her fists. "Get back here!"

Then Judy charged after Dow and jumped on his back. Georgia, unable to move, glanced at Dane, who looked like he wanted to kill Dow even though he was as paralyzed as she was.

Judy crawled up Dow's back and punched him, yelling the whole time. People were turning to look. Someone walked over and pulled Judy off Dow. He straightened his shirt and pointed to us.

"Her parents are over there. That child is uncontrollable."

"He stole my bugs," Judy screeched. "Stole them."

It was one thing for Dow to have stolen the mind-control spells. It was another thing entirely for him to say something bad about Judy. Anger flared bright and hot in Georgia—menopausal anger.

A flash of heat burned in her core and fanned out. The next thing she knew, she had burst through Dow's spell. She touched Dane and, with a flash of magic, freed him.

He zapped Claudia and Brad. "Let's go. We can't let Tarwick get away."

"Tarwick?" Claudia asked.

Georgia pointed to Judy. "Stay here with her. Your boyfriend is an evil wizard. The one we've been trying to stop."

Before Claudia could answer, Georgia, Brad and Dane rushed from the room. They wove in and out of people as they headed for the front door.

"Brad," Dane called, "where would he have gone?"

Brad, who was clearly out of shape, huffed out his next woods. "There's no telling. Someplace where he could be alone. I'll see if I can get in touch with backup."

Georgia's legs burned she ran so hard. She really needed to exercise more. "We've got to stop him from leaving. No matter what."

They broke through the front doors to the outside. The lawn was crawling with children and parents. But in the distance they made out Dow, or Tarwick, running toward a car.

"There he is," Dane called. "Come on, Georgia."

They reached him as Dow pushed the button on his key fob to unlock the doors.

"Not so fast," Georgia said to him. "Give us back the spells, Tarwick."

"Oh, figured it out, did you?" he said. "Well, it's too late. I've got the spells, and the planetary alignment is occurring right now." He pointed to the sky. The three planets were indeed stretched into a line. "No point in leaving. I might as well do this right here."

He unscrewed the mason jar. Georgia flung out her hand to throw magic on him when a familiar voice stopped her in her tracks.

"Not so fast, dear," Hattie said.

Georgia's jaw dropped. "Hattie? You mean to tell me that you're in on this?"

The old woman smirked. "Of course I am. We had to find a way to get you to search for the spell."

"Why is it that no one had confidence in *me*?" Dane said, annoyed.

"Honey, I'm sorry," Georgia said. "I was a really good spell hunter. But it looks like our daughter is even better."

Dane nodded. "True. We should hire her."

"Would both of you shut up?" Tarwick said. "Don't you even want to know our plans?"

Georgia sighed. "I guess. Since we don't have a choice."

"Finally, I get to talk." Tarwick nodded to his mother. "This is my mother. We set up the robbery so that you, Georgia, would decide to regain your powers and help us hunt for the spell."

Georgia smelled a rat. "How'd you know that I would hunt for it?"

"Because I told him that you would." Demona appeared literally out of nowhere.

Georgia's eyes widened. "You're *helping* them?"

Demona laughed. "Don't you think that I want a little mind control, too?"

Georgia pointed to Hattie. "I guess you do, as well."

Hattie nodded. "If I can take over this shack of a town, I will."

"And what was with that cookie y'all gave me?" Georgia asked. "It did something funny to me."

Tarwick smiled greedily. "It put you under a spell, and then we were able to ask you about the spell hunting. We woke you up, and you didn't remember a thing."

"But no time passed," she murmured. "At least, it didn't seem like it."

He shrugged. "We were fast."

Demona smiled. "I see that you and your husband are working together now, Georgia. I've never met Dane. Though he's met my daughter."

"What? Is Diana gonna appear, too?" Georgia asked.

"Yes, I am," Diana said, stepping out from behind the car.

Georgia slapped her thigh in frustration. "How did all of you get here so fast?"

Tarwick held out his phone. "I texted and ran. I don't recommend it."

"Yes, at first I thought your message said, 'weasel it,'" Demona admitted. "But I realize that you meant, we've got it."

Georgia shot Dane a worried look. What were they supposed to do now? Tarwick had the mason jar, and they were outnumbered. Demona, Diana and probably Hattie could work magic. If they got into a rumble, it didn't look good for Georgia and Dane. Worse, if they started throwing bolts of magic around, one of the children could get hurt. Hmmm. Georgia wondered if Missy was around. A stray bolt could certainly work a little humility into that woman's attitude, couldn't it?

"Give us the spells," Dane demanded, his jaw clenched.

Tarwick laughed. "Do you think that I would really go to all the trouble to hire your bosses, get your wife to come out of spell hunting retirement and then simply hand over the spells that I covet? No. With these I can rule the country. I will have ultimate power!"

"News flash," Georgia said. "You'll just end up very, very lonely and paranoid that your closest advisors are plotting behind your back. Didn't anybody ever tell you that? You'll find yourself single, living with your mother in a two-bedroom house while she constantly belittles you and reminds you of all your shortcomings."

Dane winked. "Good one."

Tarwick fell for it. "You wouldn't do that, would you, Mother?"

Hattie fumed. "It did take you an awful long time to track down these spells. Look, the alignment is already happening. If you waste any more time, I'll be dead, just dust. Go ahead and do the ceremony. Forget about all the others. We don't have time."

Tarwick frowned. "I would have found the spells myself if I could. I'm not a spell hunter. I don't have the talent to search for them. I mean, I suppose that I could, but I don't know what I'm looking for. Oh, I recognized the spells well enough in the jar."

"That's because a spell hunter had already captured them. Makes it so that a regular witch can see them."

"You have to have the talent to call the spells in the first place," Dane informed him. "Not every witch or wizard can walk into a forest and see the spells. Spell hunters are like magnets. Spells naturally come to them."

"See, Mother?" Tarwick motioned to Dane. "I don't have that ability. You didn't give it to me."

"That's because I don't have it myself."

"Good grief." Diana crossed to Tarwick. "Hand me the jar and let's get this over with."

"No. They're my spells," Tarwick argued. "I'll take them."

"You're not doing anything but talking," Diana told him. "We'll all be dead, like your mother said, before you use them."

"Fine." Tarwick started to unscrew the cap. "We can get them out now."

"What do we do?" Georgia whispered to Dane. "We're outnumbered."

"Wait for it," he murmured.

But then Georgia remembered that in her knapsack, the one that was tucked magically away, there might be a solution. Using her power, she apparated her own mason jar, the one her grandmother had given her long ago.

"Hey," Demona said. "What're you doing?"

Georgia pointed behind them. "What is that?"

They are all stupid enough to look. That was all the time she needed. She unscrewed the lid and pulled out the laughing spell.

"Catch," she told Dane as she tossed him the jar.

As he caught it, Georgia divided the spell into four pieces and sent each piece flying toward the four magical beings in front of them.

Tarwick, Hattie, Demona and Diana whipped around. A quarter of laughing spell zipped into each of their mouths.

The three witches and one wizard looked surprised. Confusion spread across their faces before they each burst into a fit of laughter.

"Oh, this is so funny," Demona said. "We want to make everyone do our bidding and now we're laughing."

"Use the spells," Hattie commanded between fits of giggles. "Use them now!"

"What have you done to us?" Tarwick accused Georgia in a mocking tone. "I can't work magic like this!"

Diana reached for his jar. "Give them to me. I'll shoot them up our noses."

Dane smiled at Georgia. "Have I ever told you how much I love you?"

"Not today, you haven't."

He shook his head. "Mmm. Mmm. Mmm. I just love you. Now let's get that jar away from Tarwick before he does some actual damage."

Dane pried the jar from Tarwick's hands. The wizard didn't put up a fight. He couldn't as he was on the ground, rolling from side to side in a fit of laughter.

Just then, a dozen pops and bursts of light filled the air. Dane's coworkers, the ones who had attended the party that Dane *hadn't* appeared. Apparently, they were all spell hunters. Most of them held magical handcuffs in their hands.

"Brad?" she asked Dane.

He winked. "See? It's good to have a sidekick. Even though you're not crazy about him, Brad helps a lot."

"So I see," Georgia said.

The witches and wizards handcuffed the four, who were all now on the ground.

"We're being arrested," Diana said in a fit of laughter.

"This will be wonderful," Hattie said. "Prison will be so much fun. I wonder if everyone there laughs."

"Don't count on it," Georgia murmured.

A woman who looked to be close to eighty with a pale white bun atop her head approached. She took small geisha-like steps as she crossed the grass toward them. "I got as many of the team together as I could," she told Dane.

"Thank you, Rose," he replied.

Georgia's jaw dropped. *"This* is Rose?"

Rose extended her hand. "Pleased to meet you, Mrs. Nocturne. Dane tells me that you're starting your own company. I'd love to join."

Georgia smiled at Rose as she wrapped an arm around her husband's waist. "Rose, we'd love to have you. Welcome aboard."

CHAPTER 24

"So you really think we can make a go of this?" Georgia asked.

It was the next day. Judy was off at school, and Georgia and Dane sat in the kitchen, each sipping a steaming mug of coffee.

"You mean we start our own spell hunting business? Get our own clients?" he asked.

She nodded. "You said you wanted to, and it looks like unless we do it, our careers are finished. Both of our bosses are in prison for attempting to use spells in a dangerous capacity."

While Tarwick and the bunch had been under the influence of the laughter spell, they had admitted their combined desire to use their power to control the masses—not only witches and wizards, but humans as well.

That got each of them thrown into prison. Georgia had no idea how long they would be there, but they wouldn't be getting out anytime soon. Of that, she was certain.

"Well," Dane said with a whimsical smile on his face. "I know a lot of hunters who are now out of a job. They would need the work."

She smiled. "Then we should do it."

Dane leaned over and kissed her. He tasted of coffee. Yum. Before they could get too hot and heavy, the doorbell rang.

"I'll get it," Georgia said.

Brad and Claudia both stood outside. Georgia directed them in.

Brad rushed into the kitchen. "I've got a whole list of potential clients here, Dane. All of them need help."

Dane sat up and rapped his knuckles on the kitchen table. "We'll need an actual work space. We can't use the kitchen as a place of employment."

Brad poured himself a cup of coffee. "I already went by Georgia's old headquarters. The place is empty."

She balked. "You got in? What about Toad?"

"Well, I didn't see any toads, but the place was bare."

"Not a toad. He's a fairy. His name is Toad."

Brad shook his head. "Whatever it is, he wasn't there."

Toad had obviously been in on the whole thing. That made sense since he had spoken to her about Diana one of the mornings when she went into the building.

Claudia smiled sadly. "I'm sorry that I didn't tell you about Dow—I mean, Tarwick. If I had, maybe you would've figured out that he was a bad guy before last night."

Georgia shrugged. "It's okay. No big deal, really. I'm just glad nobody got hurt and no one noticed that some people appeared out of thin air. And thank you, again, for watching Judy."

"Anytime. Now," Claudia said wistfully, "I just need to find a boyfriend and my life will be complete."

Georgia laughed. "Your life is complete anyway. You've got us. And Brad."

Brad lifted his mug. "You sure do. Even though we're not related."

Claudia flipped her hair over one shoulder. "I wouldn't have any other family. Y'all are the best."

Georgia's phone rang. As Dane, Brad and Claudia started talking about the logistics of setting up a new spell hunting agency, Georgia moved away to answer it.

When she looked to see who was calling her, she groaned. It was Missy. Georgia had probably forgotten to scoop the hay last night or something. As much as she didn't want to talk to the PTA president, she decided to answer the call.

"Hey, Missy," she said.

"Georgia, how are you this morning?"

Ugh. Whatever Missy had to say, it must've been really bad because she was starting off being nice. "I'm good. How're you?"

"I'm just fine. I won't keep you, but I wanted to say that you did a great job with the petting zoo."

"Come again?" Had she heard Missy correctly? Was she giving a compliment? "What was that?"

Now it sounded like Missy was grinding her teeth. "I said that the petting zoo was a success. Everyone was impressed. They were so impressed that I think you should run for office. You, Georgia Nocturne, should become the next Harvey Elementary PTA President."

Georgia didn't know what to say at first, but as she watched Dane, Brad and Claudia discussing plans for the future, the answer came to her.

"You know what, Missy?"

"What?"

Georgia slowly smiled. "It looks like I'm going to be very busy from now on. So busy that, in fact, I'm going to have to resign from my position with the PTA altogether."

"What? No, you can't do that!"

"I'm afraid I can and must."

Georgia hung up and crossed over to the table.

"Who was that?" Dane asked.

"No one. Have you thought about who to hire first? We're going to need a lot of help."

Dane beamed. "I was thinking Rose."

Georgia laughed. It felt good. Something deep loosened within her. Everything in her life was right. It was exactly as it should be.

She smiled at Dane. "Well, I sort of promised her a job last night, and I think Rose would be a great addition. Get her over here as soon as you can."

As the four continued to plan their next steps, Georgia's heart was full, and she knew that she was truly home.

≈

Thank y'all for reading SPELL HUNTER!

If you'd like to read more of my books, check out SOUTHERN MAGIC. Click HERE to grab your copy.

In less than twenty-four hours Pepper Dunn loses her job, her boyfriend, and her home.

It's the worst day of her life.

But when Pepper discovers she's a witch and has inherited the most important store in the magical town of Magnolia Cove, Alabama, she's as happy as a pig in mud.

Too bad the shop is a familiar pet store and Pepper doesn't like animals —not even a teensy bit. Determined to sell the shop and get the heck out of town, Pepper's plans go haywire when a local storeowner winds up dead and Pepper gets accused of murder.

Thrust into a magical mystery, Pepper teams up with a mysterious private detective and a cat so traumatized by the murder that she's not talking—and that cat could hold the key to Pepper's innocence.

Now Pepper must avoid trouble, solve the mystery, and placate her new grandmother, who keeps a strict ten p.m. curfew that's enforced by the talking end of her shotgun.

Sounds like a simple day in the life—as if. Can Pepper solve the mystery or will she become the next victim of the Magnolia Cove murderer? And most importantly, will Pepper learn to love the animals she's in charge of?

Grab your copy HERE.

Be sure to sign up for my newsletter so that you never miss a release. Click HERE to sign up!

Plus, join my private Facebook group, the Bless Your Witch Club. There you will receive sneak peaks at books, be the first to receive special giveaway offers and watch as I interview other authors that you love. But it's only available in the club, so join HERE.

And…I love to hear from you! Please feel free to drop me a line anytime. You can email me amy@amyboylesauthor.com.

ALSO BY AMY BOYLES

SERIES READING ORDER

MIDLIFE SPELL HUNTER
SPELL HUNTER

A MAGICAL RENOVATION MYSERY
WITCHER UPPER
RENOVATION SPELL
DEMOLITION PREMONITION
WITCHER UPPER CHRISTMAS
BARN BEWITCHMENT

LOST SOUTHERN MAGIC
(Sweet Tea Witches, Southern Belles and Spells, Southern Ghost Wrangles and
Bless Your Witch Crossover)
THE GOLD TOUCH THAT WENT CATTYWAMPUS
THE YELLOW-BELLIED SCAREDY CAT
A MESS OF SIRENS
KNEE-HIGH TO A THIEF

BELLES AND SPELLS MATCHMAKER MYSTERY
DEADLY SPELLS AND A SOUTHERN BELLE
CURSED BRIDES AND ALIBIS
MAGICAL DAMES AND DATING GAMES
SOME PIG AND A MUMMY DIG

SWEET TEA WITCH MYSTERIES
SOUTHERN MAGIC
SOUTHERN SPELLS
SOUTHERN MYTHS

SOUTHERN SORCERY

SOUTHERN CURSES

SOUTHERN KARMA

SOUTHERN MAGIC THANKSGIVING

SOUTHERN MAGIC CHRISTMAS

SOUTHERN POTIONS

SOUTHERN FORTUNES

SOUTHERN HAUNTINGS

SOUTHERN WANDS

SOUTHERN CONJURING

SOUTHERN WISHES

SOUTHERN DREAMS

SOUTHERN MAGIC WEDDING

SOUTHERN OMENS

SOUTHERN JINXED

SOUTHERN BEGINNINGS

SOUTHERN GHOST WRANGLER MYSTERIES

SOUL FOOD SPIRITS

HONEYSUCKLE HAUNTING

THE GHOST WHO ATE GRITS (Crossover with Pepper and Axel from Sweet Tea Witches)

BACKWOODS BANSHEE

MISTLETOE AND SPIRITS

BLESS YOUR WITCH SERIES

SCARED WITCHLESS

KISS MY WITCH

QUEEN WITCH

QUIT YOUR WITCHIN'

FOR WITCH'S SAKE

DON'T GIVE A WITCH

WITCH MY GRITS

FRIED GREEN WITCH

SOUTHERN WITCHING

Y'ALL WITCHES

HOLD YOUR WITCHES

SOUTHERN SINGLE MOM PARANORMAL MYSTERIES

The Witch's Handbook to Hunting Vampires

The Witch's Handbook to Catching Werewolves

The Witch's Handbook to Trapping Demons

ABOUT THE AUTHOR

Hey, I'm Amy,

I write books for folks who crave laugh-out-loud paranormal mysteries. I help bring humor into readers' lives. I've got a Pharm D in pharmacy, a BA in Creative Writing and a Masters in Life.

And when I'm not writing or chasing around two small children (one of which is four going on thirteen), I can be found antique shopping for a great deal, getting my roots touched up (because that's an every four week job) and figuring out when I can get back to Disney World.

If you're dying to know more about my wacky life, here are three things you don't know about me.

—In college I spent a semester at Marvel Comics working in the X-Men office.

—I worked at Carnegie Hall.

—I grew up in a barbecue restaurant—literally. My parents owned one.

If you want to reach out to me—and I love to hear from readers—you can email me at amyboylesauthor@gmail.com.

Happy reading!

[facebook icon]

Made in the USA
Middletown, DE
05 August 2021

45377533R00102